Once he left for college, nothing could convince Ansel Wallis to return to his sleepy little hometown of Hunter, CA—except the passing of his beloved grandfather that is.

Although Ansel plans to drop by the funeral and head right back to his life on the East Coast, he quickly finds himself forced to contend with past demons, long-brewing family tensions, and unexpected romantic feelings. As secrets unravel around him, Ansel spirals out of control. Just when things begin to settle, he learns just how fragile life can be.

WILDFLOWERS

Hayden Winston

A NineStar Press Publication

www.ninestarpress.com

Wildflowers

ISBN: 978-1-64890-797-5

First Edition, August, 2021

Also available in eBook, ISBN: 978-1-64890-299-4

CONTENT WARNING:

This book contains sexual content, which may only be suitable for mature readers. Depictions of drugs and death of a main character.

Dedicated to my husband Tom. Thank you for the countless hours spent listening to me rant about this story.

Chapter One

You breathe and the city seems to breathe with you. It feels like the ardent touch of a lover, cool and electric on your skin. Raindrops threaten to fall from dark grey clouds that hover in the sky like peak-less mountains. Sweaters, jackets, umbrellas get pulled out, tucked on—a choreographed dance. You sigh and the city sighs with you. Everyone is moving, flooding the streets like ants at a discarded picnic. It feels like the touch of something cosmic, for this all to come together the way it does. Even if you decided to stop, you could not change it. Someone, somewhere, would stop along with you. It is inescapable. Even when you die—someone, somewhere has died along with you.

As he stood over the open casket containing what was once his very alive grandfather, that concept was all that Ansel Wallis focused on. *How many other people in the world are burying their granddads today?* Since the casket had not yet been lowered into its freshly dug grave, Ansel took some time to pay his final respects. He had never been one to emote in front of a large crowd (much like his late granddad), so he had spent most of the funeral service thinking quietly to himself and consoling relatives. Now that he and his grandfather were finally alone, Ansel reached out to place a single orchid onto the elder Wallis's lifeless body.

Peering at said body intently, Ansel noticed how his grandfather's hands had changed. Whether bringing in a mountain of groceries, carrying one of Ansel's sisters in each arm, or tossing Ansel up in the air, William Wallis's hands were always rugged and full of exuberance. Now, they appeared different, alien almost. The skin on them lacked luster; the gold ruby signet ring William had usually worn on his right pinky was gone, as was the wedding band that adorned his left ring finger. Maybe it was the absence of these rings, or the absence of life in him altogether, but in that moment William's hands were small, naked, feeble even as they lay clasped serenely above his waist. And it wasn't just his hands: the invisible shadow of death dwarfed William's entire body.

Mind you, that was no easy feat. At six foot-two and a hundred eighty-two pounds, the man had quite literally been larger than life. Add to his size, a strong jaw, charisma, and a deep, booming voice, and you had the perfect recipe to command anyone's attention. He kept an entire room in line with a mere look and incited them to dance all the same. Now he lay motionless, all-seeing eyes closed tight, voice forever muted. Ansel also noticed his grandfather's complexion was different. Though Ansel and his grandfather had shared the same rich dark, brown skin tone in life, the mortician had heavily powdered William's visage. In death, his face was several shades lighter than the skin on his hands.

The mahogany casket gleamed in the sunlight, reminding Ansel of the way their dining table had gleamed growing up, after his mother had finished applying a vigorous waxing. It was May 25. Ansel only knew the date with certainty, as exactly three days earlier his sister Regina had called to inform him of their grandfather's fatal stroke. He couldn't believe the news at first. William was Ansel's last living grandparent and the closest thing Ansel had known to a father since he was twelve years old. Ansel's actual father, William's lone son, had died in a horrific car crash shortly after Ansel completed junior high.

Losing his father had absolutely devastated Ansel, and losing his grandfather hit as hard. Following the death of Ansel's dad, his grandfather had stepped in to help raise Ansel and his sisters. William had made so much of an impact that his loss compelled Ansel to return home for the first time in nearly two and a half years. He'd taken the redeye from Philadelphia and had barely slept since getting off the plane. He had landed in town in time to change into a black suit and navy tie for the funeral service. He felt trapped in a guilt-laden fog the entire way through.

He'd promised himself that he was going to visit when he first learned his grandfather had fallen ill, but he had never followed through. Ansel would make plans to fly home for the weekend, then reschedule. He told himself he'd go next weekend, or the next time he got a chance. His granddad had moved into the house with his mother, and she'd taken care of him with the help of a part-time nurse. Ansel had made excuse after excuse, putting the visit off the way we all do with daunting tasks, until inevitably time ran out. Ansel turned away from the casket and headed to the other end of the cemetery, where the exit lay. He crossed the street to where an old gothic-style Anglican Church stood.

The air was thick, and the heat devoured Hunter, California, stronger than any other summer prior. Ansel stood at the wrought-iron gate that enclosed the court-yard behind the church. He placed a hand on the smooth metal bars feeling along the decorative inlay. Like all good West Indian families, the Wallises had regularly attended church for most of Ansel's childhood. And for most of his childhood, Ansel had thought nothing of the ritual, until, of course, his dad died. All he could do after his father's funeral was lie flat and stare at the ceiling. His body and mind had felt completely shrouded in an unshakeable haze, a deep, dense, darkness.

Although he had been more than old enough to, Ansel realized he could scarcely recall any of the details of his father's funeral. Reflecting on it, all he could see were solemn faces everywhere, and hands extending out to rub shoulders lovingly, catch tears with handkerchiefs. The mounds of bodies all decked out in their mourning garb, wailing, and swaying to and fro in the church pews, were reminiscent of an oil spill at sea—black tides, thick like molasses, crashing into the shore. Ansel could remember leading the procession of pallbearers at the cemetery, though no one actually expected him to help carry his father's casket. He could see the casket being set down on freshly cut spring grass, and his memory went blank.

They had buried his father on a Friday. Ansel recalled this as two days later they'd sat stiffly, quietly in church as usual. Only nothing about it had been as usual; his dad was dead. The spot to the left of his mother was eerily empty. The church folks huddled in two and threes, sympathizing with and judging the family in whispers. Ansel never formed a connection with the whole church-going experience the way his family did, but that day in particular, he felt out of it. He sat glossy-eyed and spacey, detached from his surroundings. But no one paid any attention to him, given the circumstances the family had endured. That evening once the Wallises had made it home and settled in, Ansel had traversed the stairs and through the hall to his mother's room, stole a handful of her diazepam, and swallowed them dry.

The chalky taste of the pills ruminated in his mouth. As he waited for their effects to set in, he grabbed a sheet of loose-leaf paper and scribbled 'what's it all for anyway?' in blue ink across the center. After a while, Ansel felt a daze setting over him, the drugs kicking in. He promptly took the note into the guest bathroom across the hall from Regina's room. He calmly retrieved a straight razor from the medicine cabinet. He reflected on how no one in his family seemed to understand him, except for his dad, and now his dad was gone. He slashed both of his wrists horizontally.

Warm, sticky blood oozed out and trickled down his forearms. He grew woozy, and as the room grew dark, a shrill, frantic scream emanated from behind him. The next thing he knew, there were bright lights in his eyes, and he was moving somehow, while still lying flat. There was pitch darkness again, until he reached the hospital. He would later find out he had been coming in and out of consciousness while strapped to a gurney, and that the scream belonged to his sister Elise.

She dialed 911 after discovering him in the bathroom, drenched in his own blood. Ansel was kept on a standard seventy-two-hour hold, during which time only his mother and his best friend Sebastian visited him. Ansel had asked his sisters not to come. He already felt anxious and embarrassed and did not want to exacerbate the situation. He would only be in the hospital for three days and felt somehow that not having the rest of his immediate family present would make it less of a big deal. So, Elise sent flowers and a heartfelt note, and Regina sent smuggled in rum cordials with a card that read: *I know life sucks, but I hope you get out of here soon.*

Ansel appreciated them both, but preferred Regina's approach for no other reason than the fact that she acknowledged that life could be difficult sometimes. She didn't mask grit with flowery phrases or emphasize the beauty of the world over its ugliness. In the days that followed, Ansel spent much of his time alone at home. He was expected to keep his bedroom door open, unless he was in a state of undress, and could not spend more than a few minutes in the bathroom by himself without someone checking in on him. He understood why. He knew it was for his own safety. His family cared, but it still felt a lot like imprisonment. By the time Sunday rolled again, Ansel was asked whether or not he wanted to go to church.

He pondered it for a moment and told his mother that he was not up to it and wasn't sure he ever would be again. Surprisingly, this response spurred no rebuttal. She simply said she understood how he felt and left. It was the first time he had been left alone in the house since he had been discharged from the hospital, and he relished every second of this newfound freedom. In fact, he enjoyed that brief window of independence so much that he declined to go to church the next Sunday and the Sunday after that. Eventually, having spent several weeks away from church with no consequences, Ansel questioned whether God truly existed.

He weighed everything he had learned about religion. He researched countless spiritual movements and faith groups, and even tried out a few practices. He applied this same methodology to handling all other matters in his life. Whether emotional, sexual, political, moral, all choices were met with deep inward exploration and experimentation. By age fifteen, Ansel had come to the conclusion that he was an atheist. Needless to say, his father's funeral had been the last time he had even seen the inside of a church.

Yet, as he stood before the church gates, the years of unwavering disbelief skipped a beat. He hesitated for a moment, about trying to strike up some sort of deal, with God or the Devil, and corrected himself, *God and the Devil only exist in the imaginations of men.* He broke from this line of thinking and noticed a tear rolling down his cheek. He reached to wipe it away and another fell free. He waited at the gate for a moment to settle himself. He retrieved a pack of cigarettes from the left pocket of his denim jeans and stripped two smokes from the pack. Suddenly, a hand grabbed him around the waist from behind. Startled, he almost dropped the cigarettes, only to turn around and discover the culprit was his good friend Holly.

Holly was like the hand that saved him from drowning. She was funny, creative, and seductive. Her amber hair fell in wild curls at her cheeks. Her eyes were sapphire blue, and she had a pinup girl figure. She wore a tight black-and-white dress, with a big black belt around her waist, and matching black pumps. A mid-sized, heart-shaped leather purse hung off her shoulder by a long strap. Ansel handed her one of the cigarettes. She hugged him tightly and offered her condolences.

"Thank you, now can we please change the subject."

She smiled, kindness and sympathy radiating from her, and Ansel managed a smile in return. The two sat down together on the steps in the courtyard behind the church. They were half in the sun and half covered by the shade cast from the overhang of the church roof. Holly placed the butt of her cigarette to her supple, rose-colored lips. Ansel pulled a lighter out and lit her up. She took a deep, long drag as he repeated the ritual for himself. She exhaled and caught him up the last guy she dated. He was a film major named Trey, who had turned out to be less of a gentleman than Holly was initially led to believe. She summarized his personality using one word, asshole.

Ansel tapped the tip of his cigarette against the hot concrete steps below him to free any lingering ash. He took a drag and unbuttoned the collar of his shirt, as miniscule beads of sweat flowed down his neck. Without much forethought Ansel assessed that Holly appeared to have a thing for assholes. Sharp as a tack, she asked whether present company was included. Ansel chuckled and took another drag of his cigarette. All he could say in return was "Touché." Once the ribbing was out of the way, Holly opened up a bit more. She told Ansel how she expected Trey to be different. He seemed genuinely kind. She pulled a handkerchief out from her purse and dabbed at her own neckline.

"You get what you attract," Ansel said flatly. He took another drag.

"What the actual fuck, Ansel?" Holly shouted. Her voice had gone from smooth with a hint of underlying angst to shaky and filled with white-hot anger in seconds. She ashed her cigarette as she glared at her friend intently.

While Holly was well aware he had a cold streak, Ansel could see that the tone of his comments still managed to take her by surprise. He rephrased, hoping to come across less harsh. "What I meant was you have so much to offer the world," he started, pausing. He wanted to be careful, not so much about what he said, but his delivery. "You were on the honor roll, for chrissakes, and you're drop-dead gorgeous. But if you continue to put out a needy vibe, you'll only attract the users and losers out there."

"Oh, wise sage." Her voice dripped with sarcasm now as she threw her arms into the air in mock praise of him.

"I only want what's best for you."

"Well, no one asked you what you wanted in the first place," Holly quipped. "Anyway, Trey had been begging to make me the star of his next project. You know I've never been one to fall for outright flattery, but I've always had an admiration for the arts, so I couldn't resist."

Ansel took a few more puffs from his cigarette and waited for her story to come to an end. Once Holly was finished giving him the basics, he glanced up at her. "So where exactly did things go wrong?"

Holly didn't say anything right away. She glimpsed up at the sky and down at her shoes, as if searching for the answer. She took a deep, long inhale of her cigarette. By the time she had looked up again, Ansel saw that her eyes had begun to well up. Fighting tears, she eventually answered that it was because she was an idiot. Ansel paused and looked over at her. Her eyes were closed tight, in an attempt to stifle any additional sobbing. The tender flesh of her cheeks glowed red hot with embarrassment. She blinked her eyes open, and a few more dewy drops escaped. Her lips quivered a bit. He waited while she composed herself. "You're not an idiot. We all make stupid choices once in a while; it's nothing to be horribly ashamed of."

"You're right, I suppose," Holly sniffled. She wiped her eyes and exhaled. Once her emotions settled, she joked about how whiskey had always been better at cheering her up than Ansel. Next, she pulled a fifth of Jack Daniel's out from her purse. She handed it to Ansel and gestured for him to open it, pointing to her freshly manicured nails. Ansel cracked open the bottle and handed it to Holly so that she could take the first sip. She took a giant gulp of whiskey and motioned the bottle toward him. Ansel took his turn. The familiar warmth of the tart, brown liquid crept its way down to the back of his throat. He tried to rid himself of the dull aftertaste by taking a puff of his still lit cigarette, but that didn't help much.

Holly took two more swigs, knocking the whiskey down like water. She told Ansel that the worst part about the whole Trey thing was that she had slept with him. She tapped her fingers to ash her cigarette, nervously waiting for Ansel to react. After a few moments and another swig of whiskey, Ansel broke the momentary silence. "How many times did you sleep together?"

She shifted nervously and raised four fingers to signal the number.

"Shit," he sighed. He gazed up at her with sympathy in his eyes. He had now regretted being so harsh to her a few moments earlier about knowing her worth. They had grown to be brutally honest with each other over the years. Sometimes he forgot to rein it in. Holly explained herself in the frantic way one does when they feared being judged by an outside party. She reiterated that things were going so well with Trey at first. They had talked for a couple of months and had a handful of dates. Even though he spouted all of that nonsense about putting her in one of his films, she found him endearing. But things took a drastic turnabout, when she agreed to make the forty-minute drive from Philly to Trey's place in Trenton, New Jersey, to visit him. Trey kept text messaging Holly, telling her he missed her and was yearning to see her.

According to Holly, after multiple messages, she acquiesced and drove all the way to Jersey. Unfortunately, by the time Holly got to his place, Trey was wasted and kept raving about how badly he needed to screw. Ansel took two big swallows of whiskey and passed the bottle to Holly. Holly took a long, hard swig herself. She placed the bottle down next to her. Her sparkling blue eyes illuminated by the setting sun, she stood with her free hand on her hip and demanded, "I mean, what is it, do I look like a whore?"

Ansel wasn't quite sure how to respond. While he viewed promiscuity as one's own personal business, he knew exactly what she meant. She was referring to the whore archetype—the soulless seductress in tight, revealing dress and painted face, who beckons men to their doom with a single glance. "I know, right," he ultimately muttered. He estimated passive agreement to be the safest response. He was wrong.

"That was a rhetorical question. Men refer to women who enjoy sex as whores when it suits them. It's unbelievably sexist, not to mention antiquated and illogical."

Ansel agreed. In an effort to lighten the mood, he added, "But you know most men are idiots; it's kind of our thing."

"That's hardly a valid excuse," Holly answered, rolling her eyes. She narrowed them and furrowed her brow as she stared him down. "I mean you're not like that."

Ansel replayed some of the events that had taken place earlier that summer in his mind. He ashed his cigarette and took one last puff, before putting it out completely. Holly handed him the whiskey, and Ansel took a hearty sip from it before he responded. "I'm no saint. I've said and done my share of shitty things."

Though he stated this in his usual matter-of-fact manner, Holly took a moment to absorb it. She locked eyes with him. "You've never been that way with me."

But Ansel waved this off. "That's because unlike almost everyone else in my life, you never let me get away with anything." He took another sip of whiskey, half emptying the bottle in the process, and handed it off to Holly. She clenched the neck with her right hand and held the label close to her chest for a moment before she spoke again.

"The worst part is Trey's friends were still there when I arrived."

Ansel let out a groan. The sweltering heat bore down on them. He took off his blazer and wiped his forehead with his shirtsleeve, leaving it drenched in sweat.

Holly nudged him to move a few paces over, so their bodies could rest completely covered by shade. Ansel hastily obliged as she continued with her story, "So I walked in to find Trey and these idiots snorting lines of coke off his glass coffee table. He kept saying he would make them leave and we could bang after."

"What a romantic," Ansel remarked, his voice dripping with sarcasm. to which Ansel Holly nodded. "That's why I torched the bastard."

A mischievous smile crossed her face and she took another drink, finishing off the whiskey. She set the bottle down casually beside her, but it rolled and clanked loudly against the asphalt ground beneath.

"You did what?" Ansel had known Holly to be tough, but the last thing he had expected to hear was that she set someone ablaze. She laughed and admitted Trey's right pant leg alone had briefly caught fire. Ansel merely shot her a look. "Has anyone ever had told you you're completely insane?"

"Yeah, but 98 percent of the time men are the ones saying it, so I ignore them... That reminds me, I stole a ton of his weed! He was too busy desperately trying to extinguish his leg to notice."

"Two questions: how in the world did that remind you of stolen weed, and why have you been holding back on me?"

"Trey kept screaming 'you crazy fucking bitch' as I left his apartment." She chuckled. "Now, prepare to wait no longer." Holly pulled out a small glass jar, along with her pocket-sized dragon pipe, and smiled. She packed the mouth of the pipe with the contents of the jar, lit it, and inhaled deeply. She exhaled, and smoke billowed above their heads. She passed the pipe to Ansel, and he took his turn. They shared the little dragon this way for about five or six rounds before the effects settled in.

First, his nerves eased; his muscles gradually started to unwind, relax, like a cat stretching out its limbs upon rising. His thoughts, too, had become increasingly tranquil, and his eyelids had grown a bit heavier. Before long, Ansel and Holly were laughing at everything and nothing. They laughed until their ribs ached, the pressure swelling in their stomachs, as they tried to catch their breaths.

"How'd you sneak this on and off the plane?" Ansel settled himself in.

"A lady has her methods." Holly giggled a bit. "Have you spoken to Sebastian?" she added as she patted tiny globules of newly gathered sweat from her forehead and neck with her handkerchief.

"Not since he left Philly a couple of weeks ago." Ansel patted his own neck again.

"Well, he is supposed to be in Cyprus until the end of summer."

"Sad news." Ansel tried to change the subject. "See any good films lately?"

When Holly didn't respond, he wondered if she sensed something was up. They had grown incredibly close, and she knew Sebastian was inarguably his best friend. He watched as she appeared to mull things over for a moment. He figured she would want to know why he was being so blasé about not seeing Sebastian for the rest of the summer. He could feel her trying to extract the truth from him without words. She scanned his eyes for answers, but he reckoned she couldn't see past his grief. After all, grief was all he saw when he looked at himself in the mirror. She passed him the little dragon and he surmised she must have decided not to press the issue. He inhaled, exhaled a frothy, white fog of smoke, and laughed once more.

Morning came, and Ansel awoke to a stream of pale sunlight venturing in through the window to his room and an incessant beeping. He had regrettably chosen the high-pitched tone as the new alarm on his phone, hoping it would jar him awake. It worked.

At home, he had a clock radio that was preprogrammed to his favorite channel. It played Bowie, Jefferson Airplane, and the Stooges to name a few, but Ansel was a long way from his studio apartment in Philadelphia. He was across the country, in fact, in a room at the Regency Inn in Hunter, California. Hunter was his hometown, a town he'd believed he left behind for good. Being there alone was an unrelenting weight bearing down on his shoulders. Yet, the occasion demanded his presence. He had no other choice. Ansel rose from the bed.

The sheets were the same soft champagne color as the walls. The room was nice enough, neat, and laid out not that much differently than his studio in Philly, except for the fact that there was no kitchen. The heavy yellow curtains were drawn slightly. He stretched out and made his way across the small room to the bathroom. He showered, shaved, dressed, and headed down the hallway to the elevator. The hall smelled of stale mothballs, its walls were caked with thick yellow paint, and its murky brown-carpeted floors were tinged with well-aged scuff-marks. The elevator was small and old-fashioned, the kind with a scissor gate you had to close before it would start.

Ansel rode to the lobby and walked past the empty concierge's desk out onto the street. The brick three-story building was definitely no Ritz-Carlton, but it was what he could afford. The exterior was well kept and had been re-modeled to resemble a Tudor-style cottage. The inn also happened to lie around the corner from Avery Boulevard, the largest thoroughfare in the city. Ansel walked down the boulevard, taking note of how drastically things had changed in the two and a half years he'd been away.

To his right, a flood of shiny cars zoomed by a newly erected shopping center. To his left, a field of high-rise apartment complexes glittered in the sunlight. They stood so tall they nearly blocked out the view of the city's down-town skyline. He caught the bus heading uptown, in front of the local pharmacy. He got off in front of John Muir Memorial Park and walked six blocks before he arrived at his mother's home on Woolworth Drive. It was a large, white, colonial-style house, with Prussian blue shutters and a perfectly groomed lawn. Both his mother and father were descended from well-to-do West Indian families. They were highly educated, well mannered, and had all the other markings of affluence, yet were impoverished by American standards. In fact, they'd come to own the big white colonial in the first place purely as a result of the successes of Ansel's grandfather, who had been especially fortunate for a black man of his era.

The house was a symbol of those hard-won successes. It was their only heritable wealth, with the exception of whatever funds his grandfather had amassed. The house had been gifted to Ansel's parents by his grandfather after they wed. Ansel walked to the mailbox and paused for a long time. He knew he was privileged to have grown up in such a beautiful home. Yet, all the pain he'd felt during his formative years there—the sadness, the insecurity, the frustration—had never seemed worth it. Aside from all of that, Ansel had never quite felt he fit in with the bourgeois crowd he had grown up around. At first, he attributed it to his being bisexual, but he thought of how Sebastian was unapologetically gay and still fit in perfectly.

As he grew up, Ansel had realized that his feeling out of place went far beyond his sexual identity, to encompass his race, sense of self-worth, and social status. He had access to a good education, but he didn't have the wealth or privilege his peers had. His mother had somewhat prepared Ansel for this disadvantage at an early age, by instilling in him that to succeed in life as a black man he had to work three times as hard as everyone else to achieve the same level of success. However, she failed to teach him how to cope with this reality. And so, he struggled to keep up with the Joneses, while feeling like an imposter in the process. It felt as though he were a museum that contained no art: enticing on the outside, but devoid of any real substance deep within. He would have gladly traded all of that for an ounce of peace of mind.

Staring down the cobblestone pathway to the house alone was a reckoning. However, he felt he had earned a certain valor since the last time he was there. He took a deep breath and made his way to the imposing front door, which was made of solid ebony and accented with a gold-plated knocker, doorbell, and peephole. He rang the bell. He blinked, the door opened, and he saw white all over. The tiles, ceiling, and polished steps to the main staircase in the foyer gleamed in the light of day. Though the exterior of the house had visibly aged a bit, it was clear from the interior that the place was still in good condition. Ansel could practically hear his grandfather yelling at him and his sisters not to run in the halls.

In that moment, he was a small child again. He envisioned his sister Regina at the top of the staircase. He could hear his Elise trying to creep up on him, determined to catch him. Ansel blinked again and returned to the present. His sister Elise led him across the foyer. She was the eldest of the Wallis children and a successful ballet dancer. She stood fairly tall, a waif, though fragile solely in appearance.

She had the same wavy light brown hair and russet-colored eyes as their long-deceased father. She'd graduated from high school early and moved to New York City to begin her career thereafter. She reserved visits or general communication with anyone in the family for special occasions. Ansel followed her to the entrance to the living room. Before them stood a pair of red double doors and their future. Ansel and his eldest sister opened the doors in unison, and there they were, the rest of the family. Regina stood to the left of the room by the mantel.

She was the middle Wallis child, being four years Ansel's senior and two years younger than Elise. A renowned sculptor and painter, her work has been exhibited since she was sixteen. She had bold, striking features and was a couple of inches taller than Elise, though not as slender. Her eyes were the same chestnut brown as their mother's and Ansel's were. Her hair was as dark as her wit and constantly styled differently. This time, she wore it straight, cut below her jaw line—flapper style.

Like Elise, Regina lived in New York. In fact, the two had been roommates, until Regina had abruptly moved into her own apartment in SoHo about a year ago. Elise meanwhile had silently secured her own place in the Meatpacking District. Neither of the sisters has discussed why they decided to stop living together. They had seemed so close. Ansel couldn't help but wonder what could have driven them apart. He admired, even envied their relationship before their split.

In the center of the room stood their mother, Mrs. Wallis. Mrs. Wallis had been a brilliant dancer herself once. She had performed ballet, jazz, and African dancing all over the country. She was by all accounts beautiful and kind, but distant. She and her late husband had met in the summer of nineteen eighty-one, when they were both college sophomores. They were inseparable from their inception, and to no one's surprise, they married a few years into dating.

They'd had Elise in the fall of eight-six. Mr. Wallis had become a successful pharmacist, so Mrs. Wallis took six months for maternity leave and returned to dancing. She did the same when she had Regina. She adored her family, but there was no doubt that young Mrs. Wallis was absolutely devoted to her career. She became pregnant with Ansel in the summer of ninety-one, and things had changed. Elise and Regina were already displaying exceptional talents for children of their ages, and Mrs. Wallis dreaded missing out on these vital moments. With Ansel a few weeks old, Mrs. Wallis had gone on an extended leave in the spring of nineteen ninety-two, from which she had ultimately never returned.

Regina made her way to a rather comfortable, ivory armchair, with maple wood trim.

"Well, now that everybody's present, we can commence," Mrs. Wallis said.

Ansel looked over and noticed the family attorney was also present. *This is official*, he thought to himself. Ansel passed through the threshold and sat on the vacant ivory sofa beside what was once his grandfather's favorite armchair. The entire room was done in ivory and red with wood accents. There was even a set of walnut doors, with stained-glass windows in the living room that led to the kitchen.

The attorney stepped forward and greeted the family. "We are gathered here today to execute the last will and testament of the late William Frederick Wallis." His voice echoed on the phrase "the late William Frederick Wallis." Ansel scanned the room. Everyone present winced, even Regina, who was almost always stoic. The attorney unpacked his briefcase. As several stacks of paper were drawn out, the room spun for Ansel. It was slow and subtle at first, and faster and faster, round and round.

He was boarding a train again. He had never been more ready, or more frightened for anything in his life. He was staring out of the window. The shrubbery and dry heat of the town rushed by him. He was at the airport, on a plane. Five and a half hours later, he was on the other side of the country. He had landed at the site of his great escape, Philadelphia, and it was gorgeous.

It was cold and rainy out when he arrived, but he had hardly noticed. He was too entranced by was foliage lying about everywhere and the smell of petrichor in the air. It was a new beginning. He was there, and Holly was there. His sisters were nearby in New York City, but they weren't the types to get involved in his life. Ansel found himself constantly smiling, for the first time, in a long time. Then he was in his parents' living room again, staring out of the glass doors that led to the garden.

"So, he was broke?" asked Regina flatly.

"Precisely," the attorney answered. "Other than the personal effects he designated to each of you, William had no other inheritance to leave behind. I'm sorry. The good news is he was solvent at the time of his death."

"Thank you," said Mrs. Wallis. "Can we take a short break before we can go over the addendum?"

"Sure. Let's reconvene in fifteen minutes, shall we?"

The Wallis family nodded at one another. Ansel sent a text to his close friend Luca to pick him up as soon as possible. The attorney gathered up the paperwork and tucked it inside his still open briefcase. He pulled out an additional stack of papers, laid it on the table, and sat down. Regina handed him a drink. The attorney offered his condolences and shook Mrs. Wallis's hand. There was a long, uncomfortable silence. It moved into the room and refused to let up for several minutes.

Regina spoke first. "Well, at least this way we don't have to pay off his debts." She sipped at a newly gathered glass filled with whiskey and Coke.

"Oh, Regina," replied Elise disapprovingly.

"What? Are we going to pretend that he didn't favor you as the eldest or Ansel as the only boy? He hardly gave a shit about me."

"Regina, that's enough," their mother decreed in a tone so stern, so final, that Regina silenced herself at once, and a hush fell over the room.

It was a cruel joke in more ways than one. William was the family's source of prestige. He had come from nothing. Born in Barbados, William Frederick Wallis had left his home country to start a new life in the state of Texas in nineteen forty-five. When he arrived, he was armed with nothing more than a basic education and the equivalent of what would be three hundred US dollars today. In Texas, he found work in construction. Using a combination of physical strength and wits, he was promoted to foreman within no time.

William worked for the same construction company for fifteen years. During that time, he solidified a reputation for diligence and ingenuity. He was so beloved by the old man who owned the company that when the old man died, he turned it over to William. The old man, being childless and without any immediate next of kin, apparently had no other heirs. William faced and struggled to overcome the racial prejudice and social injustices of the American South during the sixties. As the Civil Rights Movement waged on, so did he.

He moved to California in the early nineteen seventies, settled in Santa Barbara, and continued running the construction company for many years. He finally sold the business to a larger firm when it became evident his son had no interest in taking over. William used some of the proceeds to purchase the same house they were standing in. Their father had often reminded Ansel and his sisters of all of this during their childhoods. For these reasons, despite any personal feelings Regina may have had for their granddad, her comments were perceived as out of line. William Wallis was admittedly a hard man to know, but he loved his family dearly. He had his own way of showing it.

Ansel looked up at everyone and, without a word, casually walked straight out of the room. He had made it into the foyer, and was standing before the staircase, when Elise noticed that he had gone and came out to stop him.

"Ansel, please wait."

"Why?" he asked.

Elise gave the typical response. "We're a family and we need to be together on a day like this."

Ansel scoffed. "We've hardly spoken in the last six years, except for on birthdays and holidays—some family." He turned away from his sister and walked toward the front door of the house. As he did so, Elise grabbed his arm.

"So, what, you're going to run away? Good job. Granddad would be proud."

Staring out straight in front of him, Ansel relived a moment buried deep in the recesses of his childhood memories. He was seven years old, and it was midafternoon on a summer's day. He had been running through the garden in a game of hide-and-seek with one of his schoolmates, when he came to those large glass doors in the living room. Standing in front of the door, he'd witnessed his father passionately kissing their married next-door neighbor. Ansel ran off immediately. He was certain he hadn't been spotted but ran anyway out a mixture of confusion and anger. By the time he'd stopped, he still could not seem to catch his breath.

At dinner, his father had acted like nothing had happened. The day after the incident, Ansel noticed his father chatting with the neighbor's husband. In his childhood naiveté Ansel deduced his father must surely be confessing to the kiss, but as the conversation progressed, he was quickly disavowed of that notion. He wasn't quite close enough to overhear what the two men were saying, but he could tell based on their body language that no Earth-shattering revelations had come to light. It was the first real instance of betrayal he had ever known. Ansel had thought about it all throughout dinner, and well into dessert. He vacillated between wanting to confront his father about the dishonesty and waiting for him to broach the topic in some way.

Days passed, and he pondered breaking the news to his mother. As days turned into weeks, he began to think that perhaps it was better his mother didn't know what he had witnessed. This way everything would stay the same and no one would be upset. *Maybe my father didn't mean to kiss that neighbor's wife; maybe it was all an accident. What if the neighbors talked it out and had already forgiven each other? What if my parents had done the same?* Lying in his bed that night, Ansel eventually chose not to say anything to his father, his mother, or anyone else about it. He didn't know enough about the circumstances or how it would affect everyone. And that was the first real instance in which he had ever kept secret.

Ansel reverted to reality. Without saying a word to his sister, he patted her hand and removed it from his arm. Elise pleaded with him to stay once more, but Ansel kept walking until he was outside. His friend Luca was waiting across the street. Dressed in khakis and a turquoise polo shirt, Luca sat on the edge of the hood of a silver roadster and waved at Ansel. As Ansel approached, Luca rose to his feet, and they embraced.

"Got a new car." Luca motioned to the vehicle underneath him, the silver paint glittering in the waning sunlight.

"Sweet," Ansel replied, smiling. He thanked his old friend for rescuing him, and a steady calm came over the both of them. Luca started the car and drove away from the house, the way he had a thousand times before, when they'd been in high school.

★

Luca's window had already been lowered all the way, and Ansel hit the power switch to roll down the passenger side window. The summer air rush in, breeze flowing by them as dusk settled in. Luca asked how Ansel was feeling. Ansel simply replied that he was fine, hoping that brevity would help to make the lie more convincing. Before Luca could say anything else, Ansel changed the subject and asked where they were off to.

"You'll see," Luca replied. The roadster's engine roared as Luca sped up. Loose bits of hair fell across his forehead in the wind. As Luca sped down Avery Boulevard, the cross-street signs whizzed by, like a mural that's been blurred before its colors could dry.

As the car slowed, Ansel saw that they had driven to the Regency Inn. Luca instructed Ansel to go inside and check out. Ansel had brought with him a single, rather roomy chrome suitcase and a black canvas messenger bag. He placed his bags in the trunk of Luca's car and got in. Luca drove toward Rosewood Avenue; with that, Ansel knew right away where they were headed. They made a sharp left onto Rosewood and found parking underneath a towering jacaranda tree. A breeze rolled by and shook the tree's vibrant violet blossoms from their branches, showering Ansel and Luca in them as they exited Luca's car. The young men walked a few paces toward a copper high-rise, labeled four ninety-two.

Luca approached the call box and rapidly entered a series of numbers followed by the pound sign. The lock on the two glass doors to the left of them clicked open, and they entered the lobby. They made their way into the elevator. They arrived at the fifth floor and approached the apartment. Luca knocked twice, and on the second knock the door flung ajar a bit.

"Come in," a voice yelled. "I'm almost ready."

Ansel and Luca walked down a semi-long hall into the living room, and Luca yelled for their friend to hurry up. Suddenly, Isabelle drifted into the room. She searched around for something in a manner that was resolute, but not frantic. Her shoulder-length black hair swished across her flawless, bronze shoulders as she searched. She wore a finely stitched coral jersey dress, accented by gold bangles on each arm.

"What are you searching for?

"A manila envelope," Isabelle said. "By the way, so sorry to hear about your granddad."

"Thanks," Ansel replied, joining her in the search to distract her from imparting any more sympathy. He searched all over the living room. There were clothes spread about here and there, empty food wrappers, and a pile of mail that had been collecting for months, but no envelope in sight. Luca joined the search but stopped after a few minutes to use the restroom.

"Found it," he exclaimed, walking out with the envelope in hand.

With that, the three of them were off in Luca's car. Isabelle held the precious envelope in her lap while they drove. They zoomed through Chinatown. The wind rushed through their hairs and set a cool blush over Isabelle's cheeks. Ansel grabbed the pair of sunglasses that had been dangling from the neck of his shirt and put them on. Luca and Isabelle thought it was a good idea and followed suit. Luca put on the pair he had attached to the car visor over his head. Isabelle reached into her bag and retrieved her own shades.

They stopped at a short, white stucco building. There were no signs affixed to the building stating the name of the business operating there. In fact, there was no indication that there was even a business operating there at all. As soon as they parked, Isabelle clutched the envelope and exited the car. "See you guys in a bit." She emerged roughly ten minutes later, wearing the widest grin. In addition to the envelope, she held a white paper bag with a caduceus on the front. She got into the car, tucked the baggy into her purse, and Luca promptly drove away.

Ansel had been away so long he'd almost forgotten how easy it was to get cannabis in California. Cannabis had been newly legalized for recreational purposes, but hardly anyone trusted that since it was still illegal on the federal level. Instead, most people utilized the medical recommendation system. All you needed was a note from a physician, recommending cannabis as a treatment, and Isabelle had one. They were easy enough to procure, but Isabelle actually had a valid reason. She suffered from severe menstrual cramps, and smoking cannabis was the only thing that truly helped. Of course, she shared with friends. *The system is bullshit*, she'd say. *Cigarettes are far more harmful, and those are perfectly legal.*

Their destination had not been spoken of until Ansel had asked Luca where they were headed.

"Oh, we're going to my house. I'm having a get-together," Luca said, rather relaxed. They made a right off Avery Boulevard and arrived at Luca's house on Valley Way.

★

Luca walked in first with Isabelle close behind, followed by Ansel. Upon entering the house, they were greeted with cheers and a thick cloud of cannabis smoke emitting from the living room area. They made their way to the kitchen. It was fairly big, with a porcelain Belfast sink, wall-to-wall, frameless white cabinets, travertine tile floors, all stainless-steel appliances, a reinforced glass sliding door that led to the backyard, and plenty of windows to capture natural light during the day. A random partygoer trounced by and handed Isabelle a beer, while Luca and Ansel grabbed their own from the massive, yet sleek, quartz kitchen island.

Isabelle casually glanced across the room and noticed an acquaintance of theirs, named Paul, leaning on one of the countertops across from them. When Paul spoke, it felt as though all the air and joy had been sucked out of the room. He was the younger brother of a popular DJ friend of theirs though, so he often got invited to parties. Isabelle informed Ansel and Luca of Paul's presence. She attempted to avert her eyes before Paul noticed her, but she was too late. Upon sighting the group, Paul shuffled over to them in his usual lumbering manner, shoulders hunched and eyes low to the ground. Isabelle blamed Luca for looking at Paul for too long, and Luca insisted it wasn't his fault.

As Paul grew closer and closer, Isabelle let a loud sigh in anticipation of what was to come. The events that followed occurred like so: The group greeted Paul. Paul greeted the group. He asked everyone how they were doing, and Isabelle made the dreaded mistake of mirroring the courtesy. Paul initiated a long rant about how much he hated his job. Ansel walked away to get a drink. When Ansel reappeared a few minutes later, he already sensed a major shift in everyone's mood (excluding Paul, of course). Ansel had another drink, as Luca and Isabelle tried desperately to contain their inner suffering.

Ansel went away and came back again a few more times. By the time Paul had finally abandoned them, Ansel had lost track of how many drinks he'd had. Luca left the group briefly to greet and hug guests who had arrived while he was out with Ansel and Isabelle. After a few moments, he re-emerged. Isabelle reached into her purse, pulled out the white paper bag from earlier, handed it to him, and smiled. Ansel and Isabelle silently followed Luca through the house and up the stairs to his bedroom. It was executed like a ritual. They swerved past party guests in the upstairs hallway who were kissing, laughing, telling jokes, and waiting anxiously in line for the bathroom.

Once they had entered Luca's room, he flipped the light switch, shut, and locked the door behind him. The light switch activated a ceiling fan as well as a bulb. They all sat down cross-legged on the smooth carpeted floor. Ansel ran his hand through the fibers. Isabelle ran her hands through her hair and rushed Luca to open the bag already. Luca ignored her, got up, and went over to the cherry wood dresser in the opposite corner. The dresser stood by a matching desk and computer chair. When Luca returned, Ansel saw that he was clutching the bag in one hand and a shiny blue-and-yellow pipe in the other. As he rejoined the group, Luca reveled the contents of the bag.

"Grade-A Mountain Kush," he stated confidently. Luca broke up the cannabis carefully with his thumb and forefinger. He placed the torn-up bits into the bowl of the pipe. He lit a corner, inhaled deeply, and passed it to his left to Ansel as he exhaled.

"So where are your parents, Luca?"

"They're visiting family in Panama for the next couple of months," Luca replied.

"Good deal," Ansel said.

Luca had finished his turn and passed the pipe to Isabelle. Ansel had been friends with the group since the ninth grade. They had been smoking together since the eleventh grade. Five years later, and there they were, all together. When it finally came to Ansel, he took a long breath and waited until the start of Luca's second turn before blowing out a thick wad of smoke through both his mouth and nostrils. They had about five turns each, before they all lay down on the floor in their exact spots. Luca got up to put on music. The first song played, and Ansel recognized it instantly.

"Really, Luca, Karma Police?" he teased.

"Cheesy fuck," Isabelle added.

They all laughed followed by a silence. Ansel lay there with his eyes closed for what felt like a good long while. When he opened them, the ceiling was swirling above his head, and with it all the smoke in the room. Ansel lay there watching it for a moment. Slowly all his anxieties and cares escaped his body. Up, up, up they went, higher and farther away from him, until they were dancing with the smoke and the ceiling fan above his head. He blinked and the next thing he knew, he was waking up in what seemed to be a field. Tall grass and wildflowers were everywhere. It was tranquil, until a shrill noise rose off in the distance. It was Isabelle. She came running over to him, shrieking.

"Where the hell have you been? Thank God you're okay. Luca, I found him!" she said.

Luca jogged over. He immediately began to laugh at the sight of Ansel sprawled out in a neighbor's backyard, with grass, dandelions, and tiny flowers tucked into every nook and cranny of his clothing. Luca calmly asked Ansel if he was aware of where they were.

"In a field," Ansel said deliriously. But they were not in a field. They were in the neighbor's backyard.

"Any particular reason you chose to pass out in the yard instead of my room?" Luca inquired softly.

"This is where I felt most comfortable," Ansel slurred almost in a whisper. It was evident he was still quite drunk from the night before. His eyes weren't focused in any particular direction, and his head was sort of rocking to and fro across the untrimmed grass. Isabelle pressed him as to why, and Ansel replied, "Because we're all just wildflowers doomed to grow among the weeds."

Though she found the sentiment beautiful and the delivery quite poetic, staring down at Ansel lying in what he gathered was a field, Isabelle erupted into laughter. This triggered Luca to laugh as well. Ansel sat up and laughed along with them. Luca and Isabelle sat down beside him in the overgrown grass overtaken by hysteria. Each of them wrapped an arm around Ansel, and the three friends waited behind the Herring house until they had all calmed down.

Since they were technically trespassing, Luca suggested they leave before anyone in the household noticed them. Isabelle rose first and dusted herself off. Luca followed suit, shaking bits of grass and dandelion from his shirt and pants, and together he and Isabelle helped lift Ansel to his feet. They snuck around the side of the residence and through the gate that led out to the front lawn. Ansel, still covered in grass, shook himself like a wet dog, dislodging debris everywhere.

"So how was the party?"

They were safely on the sidewalk. Ansel's thoughts were still foggy. His head, neck, and shoulders felt heavier than usual, but he was able to stay upright and on pace as they all strolled back down the road to Luca's house. Isabelle and Luca both shot him a strange glance. Isabelle spoke first.

"How much do you remember from last night?"

Ansel shared the last memory he recounted. "We went into Luca's room to smoke. Everything after that was a blur."

Luca's eyes widened. "You must have been pretty hammered. Do you have any inkling at all of how you got outside?"

"Nope, none at all."

Isabelle reassured him that he hadn't missed anything. They walked down the street, and around the corner until they had finally come across Luca's car. They agreed Ansel should sit in the front seat, because Isabelle annoyed Luca far too much when she did. Ansel leaned his head on the passenger side window and drifted asleep. Before slumber overcame him completely, he asked Luca to drop him off at his mother's house. Luca nodded in reply. It was honestly the last place on earth Ansel wanted to be, but he had a few things left to sort out with his family before returning to Philadelphia.

They arrived in front of the Wallis home a short while later. Ansel got up, grabbed his messenger bag from the seat, waved goodbye to Isabelle, and thanked Luca for the ride as he exited the car. They hugged, and Luca murmured into Ansel's ear that he'd be back to pick Ansel up in the morning. Ansel watched as Luca drove off with Isabelle, a cloud of dust trailing behind the silver roadster as they sped away.

Ansel walked up to the house with his messenger bag draped over his left shoulder and across his chest. He made his way to the front door. However, before he even managed a knock, his sister Regina opened it. She wore an eerie grin.

"Welcome home, little brother."

Ansel didn't say anything.

Chapter Two

As she stepped outside, Regina apologized for the way she'd acted the previous day. She dug into the petite black purse that hung over her left shoulder from a chain-link strap. She pulled out a lighter and a pack of cigarettes. She stripped two from her pack in the same way Ansel usually did. "Here, consider it a peace offering." She handed him one, then lit her own, inhaling deeply. "They're organic." She exhaled a thick cloud of smoke.

Ansel reluctantly accepted the offer but pulled his own lighter out of his pocket. Placing the butt of the cigarette in his mouth, he lit it and inhaled slowly. The taste of cinnamon and roasted pine danced across his taste buds. "Smooth," he finally uttered as the smoke gently oozed from his lips, "so what do you want?"

Regina tucked the pack of cigarettes into her purse and glared at her younger brother. "Why do I have to want something?"

"You're not the type to bond."

Regina took a puff of her cigarette, paused, and looked over at her brother. "Well, you've got me there," she said dryly. Choosing to ignore the question, she went on to ask him if he was planning on sticking around town.

"Are you?" Ansel answered, deflecting her question.

"Doubt it," Regina said effortlessly. She took another puff of her cigarette. "Mom is going to be absolutely insufferable now that Granddad's dead."

Ansel tapped the excess ashes from the tip of his cigarette against a wall of the house. "Don't you think that's a bit harsh?" He took another flavorful inhale.

"No. She ruins everything, always has. She was going to leave Dad, before he died."

"Well, he's the one who had an affair," Ansel blurted out. He could almost see the words as they escaped his mouth and hung there before him, heavy in midair.

"How do you know?" she asked. There was no hint of surprise in her voice, signaling to Ansel she had known this fact for a long while. He figured the secret was out; it was best to continue being honest, to see how much he knew. *Perhaps,* he thought, *there are pieces to the story she knows that I don't.* "I saw him kiss another woman when I was seven."

"Oh. Well, that's true, he had affairs, but Mom was no saint."

"And here I believed marriage actually meant something."

"News flash, baby bro, it doesn't. I should know; I was married once."

Ansel had almost forgotten Regina had indeed married her muse, an Italian fashion model named Dominic in the summer of 2007. She and Dominic had decided on the union while extremely drunk and awaiting a delayed flight out of Holland. The marriage was annulled approximately four months later. Though Dominic had originally intended to sue her for divorce, as a show of strength Regina seduced his lawyer, a woman named Ingrid. Regina and Ingrid had been lovers on and off ever since.

"Come on in," she beckoned. Regina opened the door, and against his better judgment, Ansel stepped into the foyer. She led him up the stairs and down the end of the long hall that led to her childhood bedroom. She opened the door and went straight to the black Victorian-style dresser that stood next to the closet. The room was dimly lit. The walls were a deep rich crimson. To Ansel they eerily resembled dried blood. It was a color Regina had chosen and painted herself as a teenager; of course that was before her brother tried to off himself in the bathroom across the hall from her. She went for the third drawer down on the left side and pulled at the ornate gold handle. The dresser drawer slid open quietly.

She grabbed a small black gift bag from inside the drawer, complete with starched white tissue paper. She closed the drawer up, stepped to the side, and opened one of the large sliding double doors leading to her old closet. She walked into the mid-sized space and over to a tie rack hung on the wall. She pulled on a black-and-grey pinstripe tie in the center of the rack, and a secret compartment opened up.

"Remember when I first started wearing men's clothing?" She fondled the tie.

"Yeah. You also began reading a lot of Audre Lorde around then, if I remember correctly. Mom was seriously convinced you were a lesbian."

"She wasn't entirely wrong, I suppose." Regina had had relationships with both men and women throughout her life but preferred not to be labeled. When their mother tried to exert control over Regina's dating life, she began dating a twenty-three-year-old teacher's assistant, whom she affectionately called Gib. She was seventeen at the time. By then, her art had begun to go on display in numerous galleries across the city. Mrs. Wallis was furious at first but speculated forbidding their daughter from seeing the man would only push them closer together. Instead, she reluctantly approved of the pairing, intending to keep them close so to keep an eye on them.

Within a few weeks of garnering this acceptance, and perhaps as a result, Regina grew bored of Gib and cast him aside. She reached into the closet and pulled out a medium-size plastic baggie, a bottle of Black Label, and a shot glass. She bent over and used the surface of the mini fridge beneath the rack to pour two shots. She handed one to Ansel, kept one for herself, and put the bottle back into the compartment. They swigged their shots fast and Regina put the glasses into the fridge before shutting it and closing the closet door. She picked up the black gift bag and opened it. Inside were a glass pipe and a lighter.

She sat down on the plush floor cross-legged and placed the items in front of her. Ansel sat down as well, facing his sister. He picked up the pipe. It was pearl white with bright splashes of red glass all throughout it. It was marvelous. As he admired it, Regina broke up the contents of the plastic bag and placed them inside the mouth of the pipe. She handed it to her brother. "Wait," she said in a stern tone. She got up and walked over to the opposite end of the room, where her record player and vinyl record collection sat on a neat wooden shelf all by itself. She picked one up, exclaimed "Hendrix!" and a few short seconds later they were listening to *Electric Ladyland*. She walked over to the cream-colored drapes and closed them.

For a second in the muted light, Ansel noticed she had changed her hair color.

"You dyed your hair?"

"Mm-hm, auburn."

They sat down directly across from each other on the carpeted floor. Ansel lit the pipe he was still holding, inhaled, and passed it to his sister. "How'd you know to offer this to me?" His curiosity surfaced.

"Oh please! The few times I did come home from New York, I remember walking past your room and it reeking of this stuff and Calvin Klein's Obsession. Not the best cover-up, by the way, though I do commend you for your efforts."

Hendrix's "Voodoo Chile" began playing. Ansel laughed. He'd tried hard to conceal his afterschool activities, only to learn now it was all in vain. Ansel and his sister continued smoking for ten or fifteen minutes without speaking. They sat there and absorbed the music. "All Along the Watchtower" came on, and Regina lounged on the smooth snow-white carpeted floor. All of the floors in all of the house's bedrooms were carpeted with the exception of Ansel's. Ansel's room had been carpeted once. Plush, beige wool had lined the floors from wall to wall, up until he finished junior high.

After his suicide attempt in the upstairs bathroom, his mother had elected to remove it. She had rather grimly concluded she'd have a much harder time getting blood out of carpeting than she did out of grout, should Ansel try this again. The deed had been done while he was still in the hospital on a seventy-two-hour hold. It was odd to say the least, coming back to find bare wood stretching across the room in every direction. It made the room seem colder, barren, the way his mind felt. Eventually however, Ansel got used to it.

"Don't you think it's weird," Regina asked, still reclined, "Mom kept all of our bedroom *exactly* the same as when we inhabited them?" The question was laced thick with energy, though she lay there serenely, her fingers interlocked and resting on her stomach.

"I guess I hadn't focused on home much," Ansel said. He chose to lie down, too, in the opposite direction from Regina. He sprawled out.

Regina continued. "Ansel, you haven't lived in the house in two years. Elise and I haven't resided at home at all in the last decade. Even when we are in Hunter for the holidays or some other event, we've always stayed at hotels, and you've always stayed with friends. Why keep our rooms pristine? Why not put in a gym, or a game room, or something?"

Ansel seriously considered this for a moment and laughed hysterically at the idea of their mother constructing a game room. He told Regina he suspected it took less effort to preserve the rooms than change them.

"Maybe, or maybe she was hoping she could lure us home."

The room tilted at the weight of their words, and as if triggered by some primordial instinct, they switched topics. They discussed their apartments, friends, and lovers. The conversation grew much more in-depth than any other they had had in years. When they were kids, they were quite close, good friends even, but when Regina turned thirteen, everything changed. She had entered high school and was suddenly more interested in her appearance and talking to boys. She started spending hours grooming, talking on the phone, and writing secret little notes to herself in her journal.

She wasn't around to climb trees or run through the garden with Ansel anymore, and everyone kept telling him she was becoming a woman. Ansel and Regina had drifted apart that year and the chasm never healed. It was as if they set sail on two separate ships, heading in two opposite directions. Now, there they were, stoned together on her bedroom floor. The album finished, and after a minute or two, Regina arose to put the needle at rest.

Ansel rose too. "I better get ready for dinner," he said. His sister agreed and Ansel exited the room. He walked a short distance down the hall to his room. A rendering of Monet's *Mouth of the Seine at Honfleur* hung in the hallway in the empty space in between. Ansel grabbed a fresh linen shirt and slim black denim jeans out of the messenger bag he had kept with him. He went out into the bathroom across from his room. He blinked and saw blood dripping from the countertop and seeping onto the floor like wet paint.

Ansel ran the faucet and splashed cold water on his face to steady himself. He brushed his teeth, gargled, stripped off his day clothes, and took a shower. After he was done, he grabbed his dirty clothes from the floor and returned to his room. He put in eye drops, checked the time, and went downstairs for dinner. The clock read 6:45 p.m. He was late. His mother had always served dinner at 6:30 on the dot, rain or shine, so of course Ansel was not surprised when he walked into the dining room to find his family already seated around the long glass dining table forking through their salads.

★

Mrs. Wallis was positioned at the head of the table, flanked by Elise and Regina. Ansel chose an empty chair next to Regina and settled in. They had all finished their salads and had moved on to the honey Dijon salmon entrée when Elise spoke.

"Ansel, you missed the addendum portion of the will reading."

"Anything important?" Ansel asked.

"Actually yes," his mother said. "Your grandfather had an asset crucial to us that was discussed, our house."

Shockwaves ran through Ansel. As he looked around the table in disbelief, he noticed the revelation hadn't surprised anyone else. "What?"

"Yes, your grandfather owned the house."

"Didn't Granddad give the house to you and Dad?"

"Yes, but the deed always remained in his name for tax purposes. Anyway, it was your grandfather's last wish to divide ownership of it between the four of us. I think we should sell, and Regina agrees with me, but Elise would like to keep the house."

"So, the deciding vote is yours," Elise said.

"You don't have to make any decisions now. Take some time to think about it while you're in town."

Ansel felt a heaviness fall upon him. On one hand, he understood why Elise wanted to keep the house. They'd grown up there. The house contained so many precious memories. On the other hand, he knew that was exactly why his mother and Regina wanted to sell. The houses reminded them of the way things used to be. The house itself was a constant reminder of how things had fallen apart.

The amount of time he had planned to be in town for didn't feel like enough. He hardly touched his main course during dinner and opted to skip dessert to lie down in his room. Regina came up a brief while later and knocked on his door. Ansel cracked the door open, but did not let her in. He was wary of her again. She had not been completely honest with him about the state of things when they'd hung out before dinner. He felt as though her omission was purposeful, orchestrated. It was an attempt to manipulate him, to cozy up to him to win him over.

"What do you want?"

"I'm sorry I didn't tell you about the house. I didn't know how to break it to you. Bad news isn't exactly my strong suit."

Ansel mulled it over but was not convinced to let her in. "I need to be alone."

"Okay," Regina answered.

Ansel opened the door before she could walk off. His heart pumping loudly in his ear and his skin grew cold and clammy as he ushered her in, but he couldn't avoid this conflict. Regina waltzed right through the door. She made her way over to a reading desk by a set of large white windows in the corner. It was soft polished white oak. All of his furniture, it seemed, was white oak.

The table stood on skinny, medium-length legs, and was accompanied by a set of elegant teal and gold reading chairs. Ansel sat himself at one and Regina took the other. They were on his home turf now. Film posters kissed the periwinkle blue walls surrounding them—*The Godfather*, *The Sound of Music*, Robert Bresson's *The Devil Probably*. He saw Regina's eyes dart around the room. She was no doubt admiring his collection. They had always discussed "serious matters" at his reading desk as kids. It was where parleys took place when they pretended to be pirates and treaties were signed when they were playing war.

"Being in this room again, reminds me of childhood." Regina's voice was kinder, apologetic almost. Ansel searched her face for signs that she was remorseful but couldn't decipher a thing so he returned her stare, unyielding and devoid of any telltale signs of emotion.

After enduring the painful silence between them for a few moments, Ansel spoke up, "I don't care for apologies, or explanations."

"Oh, okay," she said, genuinely surprised.

"Why do you believe we should sell the house?"

"I don't know."

He could tell Regina was taken aback. He estimated that she had not expected him to come right out and ask her what her motivation was for wanting to sell their family home. She probably anticipated having time to prepare her defense. Knowing Regina, she had likely theorized how the conversation would go, before she'd gone to his bedroom door. She would open by apologizing and work her way up to the plethora of reasons why she felt the old colonial had to go.

Instead, he could tell he caught her completely off guard by how frank he was. How he cut directly to the chase. This wasn't the same timid twelve-year-old Ansel she had left behind when she went to New York years ago. He was a completely different animal. He was unafraid, unabashed. It was, for a moment, like they were children again, and he had caught her during one of their favorite games, treason.

Regina cleared her throat and spoke softly. "Well—" She paused and peered around the room a bit. "—look at this room, look around. How do you feel about it?"

Ansel soaked in his surroundings for a moment. There was so much history in this room, in the entire house. It was both wonderful and horrific. His memory was flooded with little pieces of history. He looked back at his sister. "I both love it, and I hate it."

"Well, there you go. That's how I feel about this whole house. I've realized I hate it a little more than I love it. And I don't see any reason to hang on to it anymore."

"Things aren't that black and white for me."

"Well, they're going to have to be," she said sternly. She must have realized how curt she sounded, for she immediately softened her approach. She touched his shoulder and gently encouraged him to think it over. Regina rose from the chair, walked across her brother's bedroom, and quietly out the door.

Ansel pulled his phone out of his pocket and called Holly. She was outside in her candy-red convertible '67 Chevy Camaro within minutes. They cruised down eleven streets. Everything was lightning. And when they arrived at their destination, Ansel got out of the car a bit hazy. He pressed out his shirt and looked up. The address read twelve seventeen Sheridan Drive. They were at her mother's house. Holly led Ansel inside.

It was a Mediterranean-style home. The floors were gorgeous dark wood. Warm lighting filled the entryway, emitting from a combination of decorative art-nouveau-style floor lamps. When Holly was eight, her father had run off with some woman he had only known for a week. He hadn't been seen since. Holly's mother had employed an agency to track him down and deliver the divorce papers. Her mother did not ask for a single cent in the divorce, only the house. Her father did not protest. Her mother went on to become a dentist. Ansel and Holly walked into the living room. A crystal coffee table, two redwood end tables, and three soft, pale taupe sofas furnished it. Ansel sat on the largest of the three sofas as Holly vanished for a minute or so. When she returned, she was carrying a rattling green cardboard case in her hands.

"Lager straight from Hamburg." She took a shiny pink bottle opener out of her pocket, opened the case and two bottles. She handed one to Ansel as she sat down. "What's been going on at the house of horrors?"

Ansel sighed, sat back, relaxed his shoulders, and took a sip of his beer. "Turns out we may end up selling it."

Holly reclined. "How do you feel?" She sipped her own beer.

Ansel considered the question. "I don't know. I have to vote on it though."

"Any idea which way you'll go?"

Ansel laughed a bit. "Well, if college has taught me anything, it's to fight against the burdens of material wealth." He raised his beer in the air triumphantly.

"Two years of smoking hash and protesting in the quad at Walden doesn't make you a champion of the 99 percent." Her tone was stern yet still jovial. They had initially bonded over being straightforward with each other after all.

Ansel sipped his beer and reminded her he was certainly not part of the 1 percent. "I mean you've been to my apartment." He chuckled.

"Good point." Holly slid her slender fingers down the neck of her beer bottle and gripped it. She clanked her fingernails against the glass rhythmically, as Ansel went on to explain that his mother and sister Regina want to sell the house, while his sister Elise wanted to keep it. She turned to him to look him in the eyes. "So, you have to cast the deciding vote?"

"Precisely." He took a hard swig from his bottle. "This is delicious by the way."

"Thank you, and that blows, I'm sorry." She took a swig of her own. "How much time do you have to decide?"

"No one said anything about a time limit. But I'm guessing they want an answer before we have to go back to Philly."

"So, you're definitely going back to Philly with me after the summer?"

"Yes, maybe, I don't know. I mean, it's not like I've actually been going to school for the last year anyway."

Holly went on to ask Ansel what his plans were if he chose not to return to Philadelphia. Ansel had, after all, taken a job at Artist Etc., a combination coffee shop and art gallery. There were only a handful of employees, but it was the kind of place young people flocked to in droves. He had no doubt he was easily replaceable.

"You could always go back to school, do things differently this time around," Holly suggested, "like maybe decide not skip classes for drinks."

"I only did that twice." Ansel realized how pathetic the excuse sounded once he heard it out loud. Holly gave him her infamous omniscient stare in response.

"You could always do things differently, but I would understand if you chose to stay."

"Thank you. You get it."

"I know." She tilted one shoulder up and thrusting her nose in the air in the most dramatic fashion. Posing there, she looked like a tribute to a member of the noblesse, carved from stone, painted with exquisite dyes, and set to dry ever so carefully beside him.

She laughed, he laughed, and the topic of their conversation progressed. They talked about everything other than school. By the time they had come to the subject of her mother, Holly had grabbed two new beers for them both. She told him about how her mother seemed to be so upset all the time, now that Holly was taking more control over her life.

"Why is it always like that with mothers?" Ansel mused. He paused and turned serious for a moment. "Do you think she knows?"

"What, about my little hobby? Doubt it."

"Look at us, both leading double-lives."

"Yeah." Holly shifted in her seat. "Except unlike your extracurricular activities, topless dancing isn't illegal." She smiled teasingly.

"Touché," Ansel said, raising his beer in the air for a toast. There wasn't anything to toast to, but it didn't matter. They each sipped their beers. They had finished half of the dozen between them, before Ansel noticed the time. Holly offered to give Ansel a ride home at the first glance of him reading his watch. It was frightening sometimes how well she understood him. Ansel accepted the offer and got up to leave. He thought about how happy he was to be her friend. He thought about school, and his life back in Philadelphia. He thought about his job. It was chic and trite, all at the same time. He both hated and loved it, all at the same time.

Ansel and Holly exited her mother's house, as he thought about his apartment. It was small, but it was his place. The wood floors, faux granite countertops, the bright big windows on the east wall facing the street—all of it was his. As they cruised along in Holly's Camaro, Ansel thought about all he would be missing if he chose to stay. Even if his stay only lasted until the details regarding the house were settled, he would be leaving an awful lot behind, Holly included. She was the only friend he'd ever had who was brave enough to leave Hunter. She devised a plan when they were in high school. College would be her way out. It would provide her some departure from the monotony of their prosaic hometown.

She was the one who discovered Walden, a small but eminent liberal arts school located in Philadelphia. She encouraged Ansel to apply with her. He scrutinized his options carefully, and there were several advantages to applying. If he was accepted to Walden, he could get away from his family for one. He was feeling stifled by the ever-lingering expectation to achieve greatness. His sisters were prodigies. His parents had been distinguished professionals. His granddad was one of the most prominent men in the community and one of its earliest black residents. He felt he had to rise above the fray, to make a name for himself.

The day both Ansel and Holly found out they had been accepted was one of the happiest shared moments they ever had. Holly chose to major in sociology and Ansel in photography. The problem was, he wasn't interested in photography. He was somewhat skilled at taking photos and felt the need to pursue the arts, for obvious reasons. Yet, the deeper he delved into studying photography, the more his passion for the subject waned. Still, he clung to the major. He saw college overall as a ticket to freedom. *What will I do with my life if I stay in Hunter?* He grew dizzy at the thought.

Holly drove at nearly forty-five miles per hour. The cityscape rushed past them as she sped in her Camaro. The setting sun painted the sky in a barrage of pink and purple hues. Before long, they had arrived at his mother's place. Holly hugged Ansel goodbye and drove away promptly after he exited the car. He stood staring at the old colonial. He didn't feel like going inside yet. He walked around the front of the house first. Almost pacing, almost dancing, Ansel kept to a rhythm only alive in his head. He walked down the pathway and around the side of the house this time.

★

Ansel caught a glimpse of Regina leaving, as he headed back inside the old colonial through the garden. *She was no doubt heading to one of her shows.* She had been painting since she was three years old, sculpting since she was six, and ever since Ansel observed the same slack-jawed idiots had surrounded her. They had different names and faces, but they all wanted the same thing. They adored her for the sake of adoring someone. They hailed her as a genius, only so they could say they concerted with like minds. They were all trying to move up the ladder somehow. There were dealers, agents, actors, socialites, and other artists of all kinds. It was a circus. The kind of thing used to fuel more inspiration for her. She was a surrealist after all. She used to capture each of their gestures, fidgets, and fake smiles, and translate them into a completely different world on canvas.

Everyone typically asked what her pieces were about, then created their own origin stories for them anyway. Regina had commanded it all for twenty years, but he had heard rumors art students he knew that she was considering an early retirement. Honestly, Ansel couldn't balm her. He could only imagine how exhausting her success level must be. At this point in her life, Regina would probably rather lie around her loft, drinking wine and being entertained by some model. Instead, she was single, nearing thirty, and forced to attend these banal exhibition parties for work she had long grown tired of discussing.

By the time Regina departed in her sleek convertible, Ansel had already poured himself a scotch behind the bar in the living room and snuck up to his room. He had settled in on his bed and was sitting with his back against the headboard. As he sipped the mellow scotch deliberately, a light tapping fell upon his old bedroom window. He ignored it at first, but the sound grew louder and louder as a second and third tap followed. He went over to the window and parted the lace drapes to find the source of the tapping standing below.

It was a guy about his age, tall, thin, with dark hair, holding a handful of pebbles which were no doubt plucked from his mother's garden. Ansel slid the glass upward, opening the window to the young man. With one glance, Ansel recognized him instantly. It was Sebastian, his best friend, and he was standing beneath Ansel's bedroom window the way he had countless times when they were in high school.

"What are you doing here?" Ansel whispered, hanging out the bedroom window.

Sebastian stepped onto the sturdy iron trellis lining the window. "It's not even late yet. Why are you whispering?" he asked.

"Shh, I don't want anyone to know—"

"I'm coming up!" Sebastian interrupted as he climbed the trellis.

Chapter Three

Before Ansel could object, Sebastian had already managed to ascend more than halfway up the trellis. Using miles of thick, overgrown ivy for added support, he made it up to the protruding windowpane and was face-to-face with Ansel within seconds.

"I thought you weren't coming back until summer?"

"Who told you that?" Sebastian answered. He wore a loose white linen shirt, cut-off denim shorts, and combat boots. He was brown skinned but fairer than Ansel, a result of his Portuguese ancestry. His features were subtle yet striking, everything a contradiction and unbearably sensual. His hair was sleek and dark and contrasted by his silken grey eyes. His chiseled jaw led to two pastel-pink lips that formed a mouth, which appeared fragile and coy (though it was anything but). His shoulders were broad, thighs strong, but his torso was languid, delicate, and slender.

"Holly." Ansel tried to appear as though he'd not been fixating on Sebastian.

"Good, that's why I told her." Sebastian smirked.

Ansel tried, but he couldn't manage to finish a single thought. He simply stepped back and let his friend complete the ascent into his bedroom through the open window.

"Why didn't you tell me you were coming back to town?" Sebastian had now properly entered the room. He dusted his shirt off. He raised it up a bit over his face and used the bottom end to wipe the sweat from his brow.

Ansel couldn't help but notice the exposed flesh. He glanced at Sebastian and swiftly redirected his attention elsewhere. *Sebastian is doing this on purpose.* He moved away from the window. "I didn't plan on it. My granddad sort of died."

"Sorry for not being there to support you," Sebastian said. He stepped forward and hugged Ansel. The embrace fell upon Ansel swiftly and organically. One moment Sebastian's arms were outstretched, and the next they were wrapped around him, Sebastian's hands resting on the small of his back. Ansel didn't pull away either or thwart the hug altogether once he sensed it coming. He could have but he didn't. Instead, he melted into the embrace, his chin nuzzled against Sebastian's shoulder, his hands clutching the young man's shoulder blades.

He took it all in for a moment. "Who told you?" he murmured.

"Isabelle." Sebastian broke the embrace to make eye contact, "though I wish you had told me yourself."

"I'm sorry," Ansel said his voice low and filled with melancholy. Feeling himself unable, unfit to keep Sebastian's gaze, he glanced away. Sebastian for his part tried to assuage Ansel. He switched gears and pressed his friend, "What else is bothering you?"

"I don't know." There was a seismic shift in the mood of their conversation now from melancholy to a cocktail of hope and terror. "I guess I'm thinking about us and what happened over spring break."

"And..."

To Ansel, Sebastian was deliberately being difficult, dragging the truth out of him. Ansel wore his emotions on his sleeve most times, and especially around Sebastian. He knew Sebastian could read the anxiety, sensed the worry swelling and tying itself in knots in the pit of his stomach. "What is it with you, do you derive some sort of sadistic pleasure from pressuring me this way?"

"I mostly just want honesty, though I must admit part of me loves to see the look on your face, strained beauty searching for what to say. I love to watch the sweat beading your brow, your fingers trembling with trepidation as they tap against your thigh—your telltale nervous tick. I find it all exceptionally endearing."

Normally Ansel wouldn't have given in so easily. He would have tried to turn the tables and make Sebastian squirm, but Ansel figured it was better to take the bait in this instance. He was absolutely clueless how deeply Sebastian felt for him, and his nerves wouldn't allow him to let the conversation continue in such a half-cocked manner.

He sat down on his bed next to Sebastian. "And how on the night before you left—the night of my birthday, after a burlesque show and some drinks—we went to that new vegan restaurant on Twelfth Street and took the hostess home."

"And?" Sebastian's lips curled as if to suggest that he didn't know what the issue was, or what Ansel might say next.

There he is being impossible again, Ansel thought. *He can be ridiculously stubborn when he chooses to be.* Ansel knew he had to tackle the matter head-on, or they'd continue this dance endlessly. He cleared his throat. "And so, friends don't usually have sex with each other."

"Oh, come on, that's why they call it the City of Brotherly Love." Sebastian laughed. When he noticed that Ansel failed to respond, Sebastian's tone grew more serious. "So, what, I'm not your friend anymore because we had sex?"

Ansel wasn't expecting this. He looked up at the ceiling, down at the bedroom floor. "I didn't say that."He had injected a tremendous amount of tenderness into his voice, which he was now starkly aware had not been previously present. This was important to him. Sebastian was important to him.

"I'm kidding. Things are...different now, I get that."

A wave of relief flowed over Ansel. "I hate you."

"Really? 'Cause I'm kind of falling for you."

"Funny." Ansel wanted to gauge how sincere Sebastian had been, but he also didn't want to risk anything. He figured that it was best to operate on the assumption that Sebastian meant this humorously, and if it weren't all a joke, commenting on it would surely coax out the truth.

"Why else do you think I climbed in through your bedroom window?"

"I don't know. We've been hanging out since the seventh grade," Ansel said, trying to minimize it, trying to find an escape. While from the cold naked recesses of his mind, a voice screamed, *You fool! You long for this, the love of someone who understands you, who asks nothing of you, except that you love them in return.*

"Ever stop to think that I've had a crush on you since the seventh grade?"

There was a silent pause. Ansel asked coolly why Sebastian hadn't mentioned anything to him about it before.

"The real question is, would it have mattered?" Sebastian's grey eyes glimmered as they bathed in the sunlight that fell in from the open window. He laid his head down on the pillow beside Ansel. Ansel reclined as well. Sebastian was one of his oldest friends. They'd met at an especially critical time in Ansel's life. In fact, not only was Sebastian one of Ansel's oldest friends, he was also practically the reason Ansel had any other friends at all. It was Sebastian who had introduced Ansel to Isabelle during their freshman year in high school, and with Isabelle in turn who had introduced him to Luca. It was also Sebastian who had encouraged Ansel to talk to Holly, who had been in Ansel's drama class.

Sebastian had come out of the closet at the start of their sophomore year. The revelation that Sebastian was gay and proud shocked nearly everyone except for Ansel and Holly. Sebastian didn't care if it made anyone uncomfortable and refused to let anyone make him feel like he should be ashamed of who he was. He demanded respect and spoke up for himself. Furthermore, Sebastian was the first person in Ansel's corner when Ansel realized that he was bisexual at the start of freshman year in high school. It was this unwavering strength and courage that drew Ansel to him. Sebastian's wit, taste in music, and good looks kept Ansel, and everyone else for that matter, enthralled.

They were inseparable for a while at school. Rumors went about, of course, that they were a couple, until Sebastian drifted off and Ansel wound up dating Ellie Sayre. Sebastian would drift in and out of Ansel's circle of friends thereafter, always remaining close to Ansel despite these absences. Sebastian was wildly popular and entertaining in high school, and now he was lying there casually beside Ansel. Ansel looked up at the ceiling above his bed. He glanced down the walls and back around to Sebastian. Everything about him was smooth, from the way he held his shoulders when he stood still, to the way he'd glide across a room. The attraction was absolutely undeniable, but Ansel hesitated.

He posited any step he and Sebastian took toward romance put the survival of their friendship in jeopardy, and Ansel couldn't stand the thought of losing that. Yet at the same time, he yearned to take the chance, to explore this new realm of possibilities. He longed to feel on fire again, the way he'd felt the night he and Sebastian had gone home with that hostess back in Philly. Only this time, he envisioned focusing all his energy, his attention, affection, in one direction, on one body. He ached to convey all of this to Sebastian somehow, but couldn't find the right words. As if drunkenly feeling his way through a dark room, Ansel stammered, working out uneasy bits of phrases that were nearly unintelligible to anyone but himself. After struggling this way for a moment or two, he let out a loud sigh and cleared his throat. "You're my best friend," he began. "You're unbelievably hot and smart and talented, and I truly enjoyed myself during spring break."

"But?"

Ansel was incredibly nervous. He wanted to be careful he said the right thing. He sighed. "I'm not stable right now," he eventually uttered.

"Jesus, Ansel, I wasn't talking about getting married. I just wanna smoke some grass, listen to George Harrison, and fool around. Can we do that?"

Another wave of relief came over Ansel, cleansing his fears, quelling his nerves. "It's like you always know the right thing to say."

The two sat down on his bed, in his childhood room, the way they had a thousand times. Only this time everything was different. Maybe it was that they hadn't intentionally seen each other naked. They hadn't kissed each other or kissed the hostess from that vegan restaurant together. Things had been innocent between them prior to last spring. That had all been swept away now. Although they'd crossed the invisible line between sex and friendship, it didn't feel strange.

There was the lingering anxiety, the uncertainty over where they stood in the grand scheme of things, but there wasn't any awkwardness between them. In fact, Ansel hadn't felt any awkwardness during the act either. Not when they were standing in his apartment in Philly getting undressed, one too many glasses of wine on their breaths, hands and lips wandering all over each other and the hostess. Instead, it all felt uninhibited, fluid, like the most natural thing in the world. It continued to feel that way well into the following morning. It wasn't until long after the hostess had gone, and Sebastian had left for the airport, that the reality of it all came crashing down on Ansel. He and Sebastian had already said their goodbyes and parted casually, like two lovers who were certain they'd meet later. Though the truth of the matter was that they did not expect to see each other for a while, at the time a subtle farewell felt more appropriate than a more emotional departure from each other's presence.

Now, they were back in Ansel's childhood bedroom, laughing, passing around a joint, and listening to George Harrison strumming his guitar like nothing had changed.

"How do you feel now?" Sebastian asked.

"Light."

"Cool." The two young men were lying down on their backs, and Sebastian turned so that he was facing Ansel. "Listen, I'm sorry," he added, passing the joint.

"For what?" Ansel inhaled smoke. He took a second puff before Sebastian answered. Ansel propped up a pillow, placed it beneath his shoulder, and turned on his side to face Sebastian, while handing him the joint.

"For taking off after spring break." Sebastian's voice shaking a bit. He cleared his throat in an attempt to hide it and took another puff of the joint. Sebastian leaned over Ansel and set the joint down on an empty tea plate on the end table beside him.

"It's okay." Ansel was half-mesmerized. Sebastian was so close in that instant his scent permeated the air. Somehow when they had embraced earlier, Ansel had missed this scent. Perhaps he had been too caught up in the shock of seeing Sebastian, the rush of emotions that came once the shock wore off. But now Ansel savored the aroma. Sebastian smelled of sandalwood and salty ocean air. And in Ansel's mind, for a few seconds, they drifted off to the beach together, toes buried in the sand, skipping rocks across the water. It was divine, until Ansel caught himself. "Everything happened the night before you had to fly back."

"I know, but after I left, I wished I hadn't."

"So, what, you would have stayed?"

"Maybe, I don't know. All I know is I wish it had happened a day earlier." Silence ensued. Sebastian passed the joint to Ansel.

Ansel took a long inhale before resuming their conversation. "What would have been different if things did happen a day earlier?" he said, trying to hide the fear in his own voice. It was no use. Anyone familiar with him could smell it on him by this point, and Sebastian knew Ansel far better than anyone else.

Sebastian let out a sigh and rolled over onto his stomach, still looking directly at Ansel. "We would have had an extra day to figure things out."

"A whole day, huh?" Ansel mocked.

Sebastian rolled his eyes in response and left out a loud sigh. He leered over at Ansel, who simply laughed. The room grew quiet once more.

"Would you have actually stayed?"

"Again, why else do you think I climbed in through your bedroom window?"

This was followed by more silence. The house creaked, as footsteps mounted and eased past Ansel's bedroom door. One could hear the drip-drip-dripping of a leaky faucet in the background—probably from the bathroom in the hall. Ansel stared at Sebastian, drinking in his fair skin, soft smile, and kind grey eyes. He could hear his heart pounding in his chest. "I haven't decided not to go back to Philly yet," Ansel finally managed to say.

"I know, and I get it."

"All right."

"So, are you going to kiss me already?" The most vexing thing about Sebastian was that when he asked something of anyone, it was extremely difficult to say no. He entranced you with a stare, spoke in a voice smooth as satin, and rendered you helpless every time. That being said, Ansel did what anyone in his position would do: he gave Sebastian what he asked for. They kissed, but it was nothing like the first time. The first time, they'd been lost in a drunken fervor, shaky like two teenagers in the back of a large, dark movie theater. It was electric; it was primal; it was back and forth between them and the hostess they'd brought along. This time they kissed, and it felt as if their lips, bodies, minds were sensing each other; finding their way back to a warm hearth after a long, cold winter away.

After several minutes of passionate kissing, Ansel began a new conversation. "Who would've thought I'd be making out with the most popular guy in school, in this room?"

"I know, you wouldn't have stood a chance back then," Sebastian said in an equally playful tone. In his own words, Sebastian was posed to look like a model in a sixteenth-century painting. He ruffled the collar and sleeves of an imaginary smock and blew kisses at imaginary subjects. After a while, he smiled and said, "Enough, I shall depart! Good day to you, sir." Both boys laughed, and Sebastian followed up with "Seriously though, I have to get home."

Ansel asked how Sebastian got there, still chuckling. Sebastian motioned out the window and cockily pointed to a moped. He rose from Ansel's bed, smoothed out the wrinkles in the duvet on the spot where he had lain, and planted himself soundly on the wood floor. He smirked, reading the mixture of surprise and interest on Ansel's face. He moved toward the bed again, looked at Ansel, and whispered, "Maybe you'll get a ride one of these days."

He headed toward the window, but Ansel yelled out for him to wait. "Don't break your neck," he said. He grabbed Sebastian by the hand and led him across the room. "I'll walk you out the front."

They traipsed down the corridor from Ansel's room to the staircase leading to the foyer. Ansel walked Sebastian down the stairs right up to the front door. They embraced and held the embrace for what felt like a long while. Ansel whispered, "It was good to see you."

"Likewise. You should stick around."

"We'll see."

Sebastian pecked Ansel on the lips. It was unexpected and sweet and caused a smile to cross Ansel's face as he closed the front door. He turned around to find his sister Elise approaching.

"Don't worry," she said, "I wasn't eavesdropping. I heard voices, so I came down to investigate." She maneuvered closer to him and rested her arm on the staircase railing.

"Oh, that was Sebastian," Ansel said.

"That's a good reason, isn't it?" she asked.

"I don't follow," Ansel said. He was genuinely bewildered. Elise was generally not one to work an angle, or mince words. She was compassionate and careful about what she said, but still always remained honest. Yet here she was being so oddly vague.

"Your friends. You'll want to come back and visit them. It's a good reason not to sell the house, don't you think?"

"I don't need the house for that," Ansel snapped back. The veil had been lifted. *If you think your family is going to let you decide this without any interference, think again.* Ansel turned away from Elise and headed up the stairs to his old room.

★

Elise lingered in the foyer after her brother left it. She waltzed out the front door and ran right into Regina, who was returning from her art show. The two young women froze in place, as they met on the pathway in front of their family's home.

"Got a cigarette?" Elise asked.

"You know I do," Regina replied saucily. She pulled two out of the pack hidden in her purse and handed one to her sister. Regina lit her cigarette then Elise's and standing face-to-face they each took deep long drags.

Regina exhaled. "So, how have the last four years been for you?" She tapped her foot against the walkway. Ashes fell from the tip of her cigarette in the process.

"It's only been a year and a half since we stopped living together, Regina." Elise was unable to hide her irritation. She crossed her arms in front of her.

"Of course, you're always right, right?" Regina took another deep long drag of her cigarette, and with that the knives were out.

Elise scoffed. "Don't be so immature."

Oh is my immaturity the reason you ceased speaking to me? Regina demanded.

"You're well aware of the reason we stopped speaking."

"Oh, that? Come on, it wasn't personal," she said.

"It wasn't personal? See, that's it right there. You are completely incapable of recognizing when you are wrong. You show no remorse, no empathy. You're extremely reckless and apathetic. The worst part is you classify it as freedom. You hide behind the excuse that you've made it to some Zen forward-thinking place, when the reality is that's bullshit. You're a total sociopath."

Regina looked her older sister in the eyes. Elise had always been a paragon of virtue. Brilliant, talented, and honest to a nagging degree. Though, even when she was being honest, Elise never said things that cut so deeply before. She watched her words; she broke things carefully. Regina stared into her sister's eyes, and saw all pain leave them. They shone clear and bright in the light of dusk and seemed kind for a second.

For that same second, they were kids again, giggling in the front yard about nothing. In those same eyes, Regina watched disdain rise. It took hold in swirls of darkness and clung on like bees to honey. Elise truly believed what she had said. That was the first real instance of regret Regina had ever known.

★

Up in his old room, as he sprawled out on his old bed, Ansel's cell phone rang. He pulled it out of his pocket and sat up to answer it. It was Luca calling.

"I know we said we'd be back in the morning but come downstairs."

"Be there in five." Ansel hung up, rose, smoothed out his clothes, grabbed a jacket from his suitcase, and darted out the door. He ran downstairs and into the foyer. As he approached the front door, it opened, and Elise walked in behind it. She said nothing as she breezed by him and made her way into the living room. Ansel walked through the open front door to find Regina posted up against the wall next to it. She merely nodded his way and continued smoking her cigarette. Ansel walked past her and out to Luca's car, which was parked across the street from the house.

As Ansel approached, Luca rolled down the window on the driver's side and yelled, "Hurry, party at the Beckman house!"

Alicia and Aris Beckman (better known by their nicknames Ally and Ari) were noted around town for being charming, attractive, and witty twins who threw the most unforgettable parties. Their parents were wealthy and hardly ever home, which created the perfect formula for the twins to become hosts to the best events during their teenage years. Ansel got in the car to find Isabelle already in the back seat, in a glittery midriff jacket and red party dress. She strained through her seat belt to hug him hello.

"Since when are the Beckman twins in town?" Ansel asked.

"Well, apparently Whitman College went on summer break two weeks ago, so Ari has been here since. Ally wasn't planning to come down at first, but rumor has it, Ari got arrested on a DUI charge and needed someone to bail him out," Isabelle said.

This was Ari's release party so to speak. The four friends drove off into the night. In the blackness that surrounded them, the star-speckled sky looked like a million eyes watching over the city. The Zombies played on Luca's stereo. Isabelle tried to offer Luca several driving tips, which finally led him to announce that he was the best driver out of everyone present.

"Yeah, right," Isabelle said.

"I mean you drive way too slow, Issy," Ansel said, laughing.

"Oh yeah? Well, you're way too careless."

Before Ansel mounted a protest, Luca added, "Need we remind you of the Sheppard family's trash bins?"

"What? They're rubber," Ansel said somewhat sheepishly in his defense.

"Yeah, but their fence wasn't." Isabelle giggled.

Ansel stuck his tongue out at her in response. The cool air swept across the road and in the car through the lowered windows. Isabelle shivered and leaned into Ansel for warmth. They drove further down the road, rounding the corner onto Oak Haven Street when Ansel felt Isabelle clutch his arm tight as if to signal that she had suddenly recalled something. He tuned to her as she dove into the red leather purse tucked at her side.

She pulled out a little square of yellow paper and handed it to Ansel. Ansel opened it up, and inside was a note scrawled in cool mauve letters: "Do what makes you happy," it read. It was unsigned, but he knew exactly who it was from: Sebastian. They ventured further into the darkness, until they came to a Spanish-style house. It was the kind of house that was so grand it deserved a name.

Mr. and Mrs. Beckman, however, were rarely ever home enough to thoroughly enjoy it, let alone name it. Mr. Beckman was a successful banker, originally from the island of Carriacou.

He met and married Mrs. Beckman, a Grenadian beauty pageant queen, after finishing school. They immigrated to the States together, settling in Hunter, California, and thus joining Ansel's family to form the town's black bourgeoisie. They had Ari and Ally three years after they had moved to Hunter. Although the Beckmans' penchant for shows of grandeur irritated Ansel's late grandfather; Mrs. Wallis got along amicably with the couple. As a result, their children naturally grew up quite friendly with one another as well. After the twins' fourteenth birthday, the Beckmans began to travel.

They left the house to be run by the staff, who in turn took their orders from Ally and Ari. For their fifteenth birthday, their parents gave them permission to throw a party. On the eve of their birthdays, with their parents in St. Croix, Ally and Ari threw a massive rave. Their palatial residence was all decked out in bright glowing neon. They'd found a fairly good DJ online, and with no competing events scheduled that night, they welcomed quite the turnout. Everyone was abuzz about the party the next day at school, and the Beckmans' popularity skyrocketed. Over the years, they were both careful to make sure the house in all its glory stayed intact. And now in a car parked right across the street from it, it hardly seemed real.

Isabelle anxiously unbuckled her seat belt and Ansel followed suit. Luca opened his door first and they all piled out. They walked across the road. There was no traffic to look out for. Hunter, California, was absolutely desolate at night. In fact, the only other cars on the road were all parked. No doubt, some belonged to their fellow partygoers. As they approached the house, they noticed more and more parked cars. Each one gleamed in the dark, like twinkling gems in a long-forgotten underground.

They made their way inside and were greeted by Ari, who had a bottle of vodka in one hand, and the other wrapped around a beautiful girl's waist. None of them recalled seeing this girl before, and Luca pointed out that they would probably never see her again. Isabelle announced she would be drifting off to go find Ally, and Ansel agreed to go with her. They waded through the large crowd, dodging falling confetti, careful that their elbows didn't tip any of the plastic red Solo cups in almost everyone's hands. Luca meanwhile stayed behind to procure drinks. The entire place was lavishly decorated, everything adorned in marble, crystal, and gold. Inching past a wine-colored chesterfield sofa, Ansel and Isabelle rounded a corner on the ground floor and bumped right into the hostess herself.

"Ally!" Isabelle screeched.

Ally turned around, and Ansel was completely awestruck. Her eyes were emerald green like pastures, deep and rich in the summertime. Her skin, a cool shade of umber. Her lips, like two tulip petals, delicate to the touch and shaded in a calming violet lipstick. Ally gave them both sincere hugs and initiated conversation. She made it a habit to greet as many people as possible at her parties. She was always cordial, but it was different with Ansel and Isabelle. She and Isabelle had become close over the years. With Ansel, there was an air of comfort that had existed between them since they were children. "How have you been?" Ally asked, staring straight at Ansel, her eyes almost phosphorescent underneath the cool lights. He felt himself slipping off the plane around him as the words left her lips and ever so sweetly took to the air.

"I've been good." It sounded slurred and graceless in his head, but he couldn't stop it from being said. He could have uttered anything else, anything more interesting. He wondered what the hell was going on. Ally had always been attractive, but his heart had never beat so fast that it felt like it would come roaring out of his chest around her before. Suddenly things were inexplicably different. They stood there talking for a bit about how they spent their spring breaks.

Isabelle got pulled along on a trip to Catalina with her mom. Ally drove up to Vancouver with some friends from school. Ansel mostly worked, saw a few plays, and, of course, there was the threesome he had with Sebastian, but he didn't mention that. Silence eventually fell upon them. At that moment Ari appeared again out of nowhere, devoid of his earlier companion and now accompanied by Luca. Ari pinched Isabelle at the waist. Isabelle howled and turned around to playfully slap him across the chest. Ari groaned dramatically and Isabelle kissed his cheek. He, Luca, and Isabelle ran off into the crowd of the party. Ally leaned in, and Ansel's heart raced like an adolescent as she spoke into his ear.

"Want to get lost? We can go somewhere quiet to continue catching up, maybe smoke some weed?"

"Sure." *Sure? How eloquent of you.*

Ally extended her hand. Ansel took it, and they meandered through the crowd together. The house had two living rooms, one gigantic formal room, and a smaller informal family room. They shuffled and waded past friends and a drunken group of frat boys that neither of them had ever seen before. Ari's friends no doubt. When they had finally made their way to the staircase that led to the upstairs portion of the house, Ally reeled Ansel in closer.

As the crowd grew denser, Ally began using a new technique. She tapped people on their shoulders, whispered in their ears, and they moved aside for her. Soon everyone had casually begun moving at the sight of her alone. It was as if they suddenly realized a goddess was among them. Her hand gripped his tighter as they flowed from the staircase, down the long hall filled with even more partygoers, to her bedroom. She opened the door, its ornate silver handle gleaming in the light shed by the modest chandelier in the hall. She flipped a switch, and an elegant ivory floor lamp illuminated the room.

"Come in and close the door behind you, would you?" she asked, kicking off her rhinestone-encrusted ballet flats.

Ansel did as he was instructed. Ally made her way over to a set of large double doors in the corner opposite of where Ansel stood. She opened the doors and walked in. After a second or two, Ansel paced over to see what was going on. He had been in the rest of the house several times, but he couldn't remember having ever been in her bedroom since they were kids. It had a *je ne sais quoi* about it. The walls were creamy lavender with pristine white trim. Ally's double bed took center stage, flanked by two large windows, and two identical black nightstands. The rest of the furniture in the room appeared to be arranged around the bed.

A white, modern armoire with chrome handles stood off to one side of the bed, by her closet. Opposite the armoire, sandwiched between a tall pine bookcase and a miniature midcentury-style chaise lounge, sat a sizeable desk equipped with a sleek, rolling computer chair. Ansel took his shoes off and traipsed across the plush, tan carpet to where the closet doors stood. The floor was somehow softer than any other carpet he could ever remember encountering. Ally opened the closet and entered it, leaving the doors slightly ajar. Ansel peered in after her and discovered the closet was roughly the size of a small child's bedroom.

"It's big, I know." Ally smiled. She exited the closet carrying a two-foot bong in her left hand, a silk pouch, and some sort of little remote in the other hand. "Sorry for dragging you up here. I needed to get away for a moment."

"No worries. I know how that feels."

"Right, didn't you just get in from Philadelphia?"

Ansel simply nodded in response. She eyed him, but in a manner that didn't feel too intrusive. "What brings you back?" she asked. There was no judgment in her voice, only curiosity. She eased down onto her bed, seated upright but comfortable, with the bong balanced between her thighs. She had been wearing her hair pinned in an updo and decided to unfasten the hairpins. A dark brown lustrous wave cascaded down to her shoulders.

"My granddad died, so I flew in for the funeral."

"I'm so sorry to hear that."

He had heard that phrase or some variation thereof from practically everyone he came in contact with since his grandfather's funeral. He knew what the words meant, what everyone was trying to convey through them, but they had begun to wear on him. They'd started to lose all their luster, all of their intended power. *What do they all have to be so sorry about?* It wasn't like his grandfather was murdered. It was like any of them were responsible for the stroke that killed the man. *I'm so sorry*—Ansel had started to despise those words and everyone who had spoken them.

So, of course, it took him entirely by surprise when he did not feel that same sense of revulsion toward Ally after she'd said them. Perhaps it was because when others had uttered the phrase, it always both sounded and felt a bit disingenuous. It was as though they didn't know what else to say and were coerced by everyone around them into offering infinite apologies, because that's what one does when there's been a death. Yet, when Ally said it there was no rehearsed pity or regret attached, no coerced sympathy, just real live empathy. Her eyes lit up, and she stretched out to lay her hand on his forearm. It was the second time she had randomly reached out to touch him. At first, he began to read into it, but he cogitated and realized she was sort of a touchy-feely person in general.

She enjoyed making intimate contact with everyone when expressing herself. To her, it was as satisfying as discovering a source of light in perpetual darkness. Still, a nagging part of Ansel couldn't avoid feeling like he had said too much. He lamented not saying something vaguer like, *Oh, I'm here visiting family*. That's the type of thing one says in these situations to minimize the impact, but it was too late; he had already crossed the line.

"Ah, it's all right," Ansel started trying to remain cool on the outside, while on the inside his mind scrambled for something to say to soothe the awkwardness. "He wasn't in good shape before the end came, so we had a lot of time to prepare."

"I remember when our nana passed it was the same way. She was so sick. It was almost a relief to see her go." Ally gently lifted her hand from Ansel's shoulder.

He pondered on how long she had left it there. He now knew exactly why it felt so different when Ally had offered her condolences; she was speaking from experience. The thought filled him with a gnawing excitement, though he did his best to contain himself, retain his composure.

She walked over to the far side of the room, opened one of the windows, and sat down cross-legged on her canopy bed. She motioned for him to join her. Noticing his reluctance, she added in a mocking tone, "Ansel Wallis, I hereby grant thou permission to sit on my bed."

He laughed, walked over, and plopped down on the bed beside her.

"You have an infectious laugh," she noted, handing him the bong along with a lighter. He thanked her sheepishly, in acceptance of both the compliment and the bong. He gripped the neck of the latter with one hand, while he held on to the lighter Ally had passed him with the other.

"This is top shelf; it's called Ambrosia." She was sitting at a decent distance from Ansel, not too close, but not too far away. She reached over to the end table nearest to her and picked up a tiny remote control. She pressed the power button and music flooded into the room.

Ansel lit and took a deep, long pull from the bong. He sat motionless, blowing out smoke as the music filled him down to his marrow. He passed the bong to Ally. "What is this beautiful language?" he asked after a few seconds of trying to decipher it. It sounded like French mixed with a bit of German, and yet also distinctly different from those two tongues.

"It's Swedish," she said before taking her own turn with the bong. Smoke billowed from parted lips, encasing her in a dream-like cloud. "You know," she started, as the cloud began to dissipate. She gazed at him intently, soaking in all of his features—eyes, hair, nose, mouth, and her gaze reached beyond that, beyond his flesh altogether. "There's something innately cool about you," she said finally.

"That's funny." He relaxed. "I could say the same about you."

"Aw, shucks." She smiled wide. "You're being too sweet."

He didn't reply. Despite being born and raised in Hunter, Ansel had always felt like an outsider there. She was his antithesis in that regard. He took another turn and passed the bong to her.

She grabbed it from him. "Sometimes I get so wrapped up in all the downsides of everything, you know?"

"Oh yeah, it has to be difficult getting everything you want," Ansel said. He had meant it jokingly, but he realized how it might have sounded to her. He scanned her face for a tell, the slightest hint of how she was going to react. He realized in that moment that he knew her, but he didn't *know* her.

"Ha!" she said. "But it is. There are no challenges. It feels...empty sometimes."

First relief settled over Ansel; then he absorbed her statement and nodded. He wanted to say that he'd experienced firsthand how lonesome, and maddening, and ravenous that emptiness was, but he decided it was better not to reveal too much of himself. At least not yet.

"It's silly. I used to love my little world here—the parties and everything, but now I don't know. I feel like it all sort of wore off after being away at school for the last two years. Living in Washington has taught me that there's so much more to life." She shifted toward him, as if awaiting his thoughts on the matter. Several strands of her silky hair fell across her face. She brushed them back casually. "Is that how you felt in Philadelphia?" she asked.

She must have realized he hasn't said anything. He hadn't responded. He didn't quite know how to answer the question. His first two years were unlike anything else. He had been sheltered in high school, all throughout his life. His parents were yuppies, so they dressed him accordingly, and he hated it. He hated his entire identity as he knew it back home, save for the small group of friends who understood him. College was his chance to break free, reinvent himself, and so he'd done that. His first two years in college Ansel hung out with neo-hippies. He routinely skipped classes on a whim, with the exception of philosophy and photography. He smoked copious amount of cannabis, ran late without a worry, danced all night, and dropped acid in the woods. They were marvelous experiences that he would never forget, but of course he didn't share all of that with Ally.

"It was different for me."

"I suppose it's different for everyone." She slid in close to him, close enough to touch without touching. "How has it been for you, being back here?"

No one he had spoken to since his return had asked him, not even Holly. The bulk of his conversations were all condolences and small talk carefully curated to avoid upsetting him. "It's been strange," he said, examining his feelings "I've only been here for a few days and already everyone has expectations."

"Some want you to stay, some want you to go," she said, waving her hand in the air sideways. She used her hands a lot to express herself. She did it gracefully, like a conductor. The world was her orchestra, every story her symphony.

"Exactly." Ansel couldn't help but agree, He was mesmerized by her, lost in her gestures.

"I love my life in Hunter, but I find it hard to leave Walla Walla. I enjoy getting to be someone different when I'm away from home."

Ansel knew exactly what she meant. "You get to recreate yourself, start fresh." He had not noticed, but he had been staring off into nothingness for several seconds. By the time he looked at her, the most serene expression had crossed Ally's face.

"Exactly," she said. And no more words were shared between them for a little while. They took turns smoking and enjoying Ally's music. "I'm stoned as shit," she said, breaking the silence. They both erupted into laughter. She casually reached into her pocket and pulled out a little vial half-filled with pristine white powder. "Wanna do a bump?" she asked.

He froze. He had never done cocaine before but wanted desperately to impress her. He hated himself for it, for wanting to impress anyone so badly that he would dive into doing cocaine, but it was the truth. Besides it was only a small amount, only a bump, he silently reasoned with himself. *What am I to do anyway, decline? No, declining is not an option.* Declining would have been social suicide, not to mention that he did not want to miss out on the opportunity to bond with Ally in this way.

"Sure," he said, trying to sound cool after what felt like much too long of a pause. Ally retrieved what looked like a tiny crochet needle from her pocket and tapped a bit of coke onto the end of it. She went first, offered it to Ansel. Ansel mimicked Ally and closed off his right nostril with an index finger. He inhaled deeply from the tip of the apparatus as she had done. Within moments he felt a raw burst of energy rush through him. It was as if lightning had struck him right in the spine. "Hey, I have an idea," he blurted out. "Do you want to get out of here for a bit?" he asked. He was nervous yet simultaneously confident somehow.

"Sure," she said. She placed the bong down on the end table beside her and smoothed out her clothes before rising to her feet.

Ansel noticed that there did not seem to be an ounce of ambiguity in her voice when she agreed to leave with him. There was no rethinking it, no prudent examination of her diction. She said what she wanted, and it came out sounding as cool as ever. This time, Ansel extended his hand and guided her out of the room. Her palm gripped his tightly as they meandered around party guests and down the long corridor to the stairs. Ally almost tripped at one point, over an empty red plastic cup, but Ansel swiftly caught her at the waist in time to save her from hitting the ground.

"Thank you, that would have been quite embarrassing," she whispered in his ear, to avoid having to shout over the thumping music.

Weaving through even more guests, they eventually arrived at the kitchen. Someone groggily shouted Ansel's name, and he used his free hand to wave at them. Nearly everyone in the kitchen was drunk. Random people kept stopping to touch Ally's shoulder, say hello, or blow her a kiss. *What a goddess.* Once they had made it across the kitchen to the door leading to the backyard, Ally paused and asked him to wait with a sudden sense of urgency. She took off back into the crowd but was only gone for a minute or two before she returned holding a lanyard.

"Had to grab my keys," she said, jingling them in the air above her head. They exited the kitchen, flowed past guests in the backyard, until they came to a giant wooden side gate. He propped the gate open as Ally pranced onto the sidewalk. He joined her and they were off. They strolled off the sidewalk out into the open road. The darkness of night cloaked everything around them. They passed by Luca's car and all the other cars parked outside.

There was a ubiquitous air of freedom in leaving the party by themselves without any particular destination in mind. Being back in Hunter felt like watching his past in Technicolor. She must've felt that way too, in spite of the fact that she loved her life here. Being high and drunk enough that his usual inhibitions were almost nonexistent, Ansel came out asked a question that had come to mind. "Kind of feels like you're leaving your past self at the party, right?

"Yes," she exclaimed. "I couldn't put my finger on it when I first got back, but now I know. It feels more like there's two of me: the Ally everybody here in Hunter knows, and the person I am now." They strolled further underneath the sycamore trees that lined the road. The trees grew taller and wider, and their branches hung so low they nearly grazed Ansel's and Ally's heads. The half-faced moon stuck, shining, grinning down on them.

Ansel shivered. It had grown noticeably colder than when he had arrived at the party and much breezier now. He stepped in closer to Ally, who stood to the right of him. She flung her arms around him dramatically. "Do you need my jacket?" she offered, half laughing. Shuffling beside her out in the night air, for the first time that evening, Ansel smelled the scent of Ally's perfume. There were notes of jasmine and honeysuckle, sweet and mellow. Their hands brushed against each other for a moment. Ally waltzed sideways.

"I would take it, if you were wearing one," he quipped. Another cold breeze rolled by, and Ansel tucked his hands into his pants pockets.

"Touché." Her words echoed louder in the night than she had anticipated. It was startling, but she laughed it off. "God, it feels good to yell!" she added. Ally placed her hand in the crook of Ansel's arm and leaned into him for a moment.

"It really does!" he responded in a shout to match hers.

They both laughed this time. She turned to look at him, and in the most serious tone he had heard from her all night she asked a question he had not been prepared to answer. "Why did you choose to go to school in Philadelphia?"

He paused, thinking it over carefully. "Well, what made you choose to go to school in Washington?" he countered. He meant this earnestly. He was not trying to deflect, but after he'd said it, he realized it could've been interpreted that way. He debated saying something further but decided not to. Instead, he waited, hoping to relate to whatever she said next.

"I wanted to get away, but I also longed to be somewhere near an assortment of trees. I grew up constantly surrounded by sycamores here in Hunter, and always loved that. But I ached for new land filled with trees. Walla Walla was about an hour away by plane, which is the right amount of distance from home."

Ansel completely understood. "Who-a-who-a?" he jested, devoid of anything else to add. She laughed, which made him feel rewarded. She warned him not to rag on her town. She enjoyed living there and preferred it to dealing with hustle and bustle of a big city like Seattle. Walla Walla was modest and the people were sweet and genuine. "I don't know, maybe I'm being pretentious," she mused.

He paused. "Not that you need my approval, but I don't think so." *The right amount of distance*—those words resonated with him. Maybe it was the booze, the hit of coke, or the cold, but before he knew it Ansel started spilling his insides. "I chose Philly for the distance too," he continued. "I wanted to be as far away as possible. I guess my life was always so complicated here, and I was so tired of it all after high school." He paused. He would have feared he had said too much, but he was still too high to care. "That and I always thought there were way too many damn trees here!"

"You're crazy," she said, amused, "and what was so complicated about your life? Your family seems pretty normal. In fact, from what my parents have said, the Wallises are known as a well-to-do clan in the islands."

"For lack of a better cliché, looks can be deceiving. All we have is our reputation."

"A reputation for success." She playfully nudged him in the ribs with her elbow.

"Yeah, my family does, not me." Ansel removed his right hand from his pocket and slid it across his chest as if repeating a pledge. "I'm not a genius, just raised in a house full of them," he added. He had said it in a self-deprecating manner, meant as a cynical joke, but the words hung in the air menacingly. He slipped his hand back into his pocket, and as he did Ally latched her arm into the crook of his again.

"So, you're not even the least bit spoiled?" She completely glossed over the stony comment, unfazed as they strolled along.

"I wouldn't say so. My mom is only paying for my education, or what grants don't cover anyway. It's not like I have a trust fund or anything. I've had a job since I was seventeen, and I pay my own rent and utilities back in Philly."

"Oh," she said in a way that sounded a bit defeated, yet devoid of resentment, "well, even though I can't entirely relate, I understand where you're coming from."

"Good enough for me," he said. They smiled at each other, a deep warm smile, and walked a few steps further into the dark.

"I bet you were popular with the girls in Philly."

"Not in the least." He chuckled.

"Seriously? I don't believe it. Even with that charming smile?"

"To be honest, I'm kind of shy and the girls I have approached either don't date black guys, or bisexual guys for that matter." *Shit! Wait, why did I say that?* Ansel thought. *I mean it's true, but is she flirting with me? She is definitely flirting with me.*

"Pity. I've never experienced that with a guy, but I guess guys are less picky. Either that or they fetishize me for being West Indian."

"Oh God, I hate that. I used to get that a lot here actually. 'You're so exotic.' As if we become a special kind of black."

"I know," she groaned, her face momentarily mired in an expression of pure irritation. "The hint of European blood in our heritage does not deem us worthy of respect. You should respect us anyway."

"Yes," he cried out.

She turned toward him, placed a hand on each of his shoulders, and gave them a little squeeze. "Ugh," she cried out in relief. "Sorry, I've never met anyone in Hunter who is honest about these things." She was facing him, staring him straight in the eyes, staring right through him as she released her grasp.

Ansel gripped her palm with his as her arms fell languidly at her side, and they strolled forward together hand in hand. "No, it's all right," he said. "I understand completely."

Ally nodded, and they walked a few paces further down the road, before ultimately deciding to turn back. Another breeze swept through, and it made Ansel think of

Philadelphia. He reminisced about walking to the street to catch a cab from his apartment building. There was always a play, concert, or cabaret waiting downtown. He imagined walking passed old Mrs. Hanley at the corner deli.

He could practically see the clerk from Stevenson's market, bent over a porno mag as usual, trying to be inconspicuous about it at the bus stop. He recalled the rainy autumns, shuffling through crowded sidewalks, barely clinging to his umbrella. The cold snowy winters that left the pavement slick with snow and sleet, and, of course, the way the entire city lit up at night in the summer. He thought about the version of himself that everyone knew here in Hunter, and how it contrasted to the person he truly was now. He was convinced that he couldn't give the latter up, not even for all the trees in Walla Walla. They strolled toward the parked cars again, walked up to the house. Once inside, they found that the party had started to die down.

People were sprawled out and seated on all kinds of surfaces: sofa arms, countertops, the floors, the staircase. Ansel looked around, but only identified a few people. The Beckmans' parties had been a gathering of young people who partook in alcohol and drugs, yes, but they were pursuing something greater than that, greater than themselves—freedom. Some of these kids didn't get into art schools in Philly or have the privilege of choosing Whitman College from among their many acceptances. Some of them were still here in their hometown, working at the mall. Almost every youth in Hunter worked at the mall at some point, whether in some clothing store or gift shop. And if not at the mall, they worked at the local movie theaters or populated the grocery markets.

Hunter, by and large, was a town of people who only ever moved a few miles from their parents. It was one of the many reasons Ansel felt compelled to escape it. He would've bet anything that his fellow expatriates shared the sentiment, until he spoke to Ally tonight. She was an anomaly; she had mixed feelings. She loved Hunter, but she also loved being away. She couldn't explain it, and he didn't feel the need for her to. Ansel didn't feel like he would ever advance in Hunter. *Is that what it is? God, yes.*

He remembered the summer before eighth grade, the summer his father died. It was hot and sticky outside all day. The kind of summer where you're drenched in sweat without moving an inch. Everyone wore sleeveless shirts and shorts and sandals. Businessmen exiting from the air-conditioned buildings downtown vainly patted their foreheads with satin handkerchiefs at first exposure to the heat. Deciding he needed a change after everything that had happened, Ansel had shaved his head. On the first day of school, his friends commented on how new and cool it was. Later that day, while strolling through the halls, he heard two kids mocking him.

"He thinks he's so original," one boy said.

"Who, suicide boy? Yeah, what a dickwad," the other one chimed in.

The nickname devastated him. Ansel had been trying to start fresh, trying to establish himself at a new school in a new grade, as a new person, but it was too late. Everyone was already aware of who he was, the brother of two genius artists, the boy who had tried to off himself after his father died. Of course, he had not been wholly naïve. He figured that word of his attempt to take his own life would spread like wildfire during summer break, as tragic events tend to do in small towns like Hunter. But hearing someone talk about him firsthand, hearing himself be referred to as "suicide boy," was different. It almost broke him.

He went home and obsessed over it, thinking of clever things he could have said or done in response, *l'esprit d'escalier*. After pondering for hours, Ansel settled on the conclusion that the boys simply didn't understand change. It bothered them, made them uncomfortable. He realized nothing had changed in the entire town, for as long as he could remember. It angered him completely and utterly.

He went to school the next day and strolled through the halls quietly, eyes live behind dark sunglasses. He passed one of the two boys he had overheard talking about him the previous day. It was the worst of the two. The boy stopped Ansel and facetiously noted what an improvement Ansel's new look was. When Ansel didn't reply, the boy referred to him as an *uppity nigger*. With a crowd of eyes surrounding them, Ansel replied by hitting the boy square in the jaw. The boy took a couple of steps backward, gazing at Ansel. He was scared and confused as blood ran down his lip to his chin. Nobody around them said a word, and from that day forward no one took jabs at "suicide boy" out loud ever again. In that moment, Ansel was mysterious and cool. He was calm and collected one minute, and unpredictable the next.

Rumors about him began to swirl. The whispers made him exciting and a bit dangerous. It made him reckless. *Why stop when you don't have anything to lose?* But that air of mystery wasn't enough to cloak him forever. He had to leave, had to get to a place where he could finally breathe. Going to college in Philly solved that. The air felt heavy, and the streets were dense with history at home. Failures, miseries, happiness, and expectations waited for him around every corner. Though he was still uncertain about whether he'd return to school, or whether he'd return to Philly at all, Ansel was sure of one thing: his future did not lie in Hunter, California.

Chapter Four

He awoke the next morning to the sun cascading in through the slightly drawn drapes in Luca's room. He was lying tucked into a sleeping bag on the floor with zero recollection of how he'd gotten there. The last thing Ansel did remember was returning to the Beckman house with Ally and hugging her before she was whisked off by one of her other party guests. From there everything was like a Gaussian blur. He closed his chestnut eyes, but saw only pieces of imperceptible images floating by, in between the flashes of bright red flesh, the insides of his eyelids. He felt a considerable, dull ache behind his temples. A hangover, no doubt, but not of the staggering, all-consuming variety.

Luca waltzed into the room in plaid drawstring shorts and a plain white T-shirt. "Rise and shine, pretty boy," he whispered, nudged Ansel with the edge of his foot.

"Already awake," Ansel managed to mumble, before the ache rang out between his eyes.

"Breakfast?"

"Yes, please."

Luca nodded and headed to the kitchen. Ansel lay on his back for a moment, staring at the ceiling, gathering himself. Like Luca, Ansel wore drawstring shorts, but the ones Ansel had on were black gym shorts with "Hunter High" printed in big white letters across the left thigh. He didn't remember much, but he knew Luca had loaned the shorts to him. He wore a gossamer white, long-sleeved, collared shirt over the shorts, a remnant of his outfit from the night before. He folded the sleeping bag in half and followed Luca down to the kitchen.

On the way, Ansel couldn't help but notice how tidy the house now was. Everything was spic and span—bleached, dusted, and swept to perfection. When he got to the kitchen, he found Luca preparing breakfast on the island. Ansel walked over to it. Elegant leather bar stools with low backs lined the side of the island nearest to him. He pulled out a stool and slouched back as far as he could. Ansel hadn't remembered seeing the stools his first night in town at Luca's, but immediately figured his friend must've tucked them away to save space. Luca moved through his immaculate surroundings with the prudence and agility of a trained spy.

He cracked four eggs over a clear glass bowl, whisked them together for a minute, and seasoned the mix. He selected a heavy skillet and a bamboo cutting board from one of the cupboards underneath the island. Luca placed the skillet on the nearby stove and poured half of the egg mixture from the glass bowl into it. Almost like a reflex, he wiped the thick oozing yolk that split from the edge of the skillet.

Ansel sat up to better assess things. "Your mom coming home soon?"

"Three days from now. Figured I might as well get a head start on cleaning. Anyway, where did you run off to last night?"

"I didn't run off," Ansel answered. He casually crossed his arms, in an unconscious act of self-defense. "I walked off."

"Mhmm, with your girlfriend Ally."

Ansel shushed him. "She's not my girlfriend and nothing happened."

"Why are being so secretive? No one's even here." Luca raised an eyebrow. He walked over to the refrigerator. It was a behemoth, with double doors, resting atop a roomy, bottom-drawer freezer. Luca retrieved two sausages from one of the fridge doors and brought them over to the cutting board.

Ansel shifted uneasily in his seat. He started to speak but stopped himself abruptly, unable to find the right words to properly describe the situation.

With Ansel set on remaining silent, Luca finally spoke up. "It is impossible for nothing to have happened. If nothing happened, you guys took off somewhere and immediately passed out. And even then, that's something"" Luca began to chop sausages. He signaled to Ansel to grab some bread from the loaf sitting nearby on the island.

"And I thought I was the philosophy nerd." Ansel opened the plastic overwrap, grabbed four slices of bread, and tied a knot in the plastic to close it back up. He loaded Luca's toaster with two of the slices.

Luca finished chopping and dispersed the sausage bits into the skillet atop the egg mixture. "Don't you have to actually go to class to be a nerd?" he quipped. He turned the stove on and lowered the flame.

"Ouch," Ansel said. He also couldn't help but laugh at the friendly dig. "I'd like to tell you we went on some great adventure, but we took a walk down the street and talked about school."

"That sounds lovely," Luca replied. He produced two forks from a drawer built into the island and grabbed two terracotta-style bowls from one of the wall cabinets above the sink. He placed the bowls and utensils down on the counter next to the skillet, scooped the contents of the skillet into his chosen bowl. "Can I ask you something?" he said.

"Sure," Ansel said. *Whap!* The toast exited, well browned on both sides. Ansel handed the finished slices to Luca and placed the second pair in the still hot toaster.

"You mentioned school, but you're not going anymore. What about that?"

"Of course, I didn't tell Ally I dropped out. We don't know each other well enough for me to trust her with a secret like that."

"And your family?"

"Haven't told them yet either. Apparently, my granddad was the actual owner of our house, and when he died, he left it to the four of us: my mom, Regina, Elise, and myself. Now my mom and Regina want to sell the house, but Elise wants to keep it."

"Shit," Luca said while munching away at his eggs. "If you sell?" he managed to add in between bites. The scraping of the fork across his plate echoed in the air.

"If we sell, I can go back to Philly, back to smoking out in my apartment with Holly," Ansel said. He took a bite of toast and forked some of the eggs into his mouth along with it. He swallowed, added, "I'd keep my job at the gallery, but I'd be set for a while. Hell, I might even re-enroll in school."

"And if you stayed?"

Whap! The second pair of toast was done. Ansel grabbed it and placed the piping-hot bread down on a waiting plate. "Well, I get to see you guys more, and Sebastian, of course. But I wouldn't have anywhere to live except my mom's house, which she'd be keeping begrudgingly."

As the boys finished eating, they heard a knock at the front door. Luca went to see who it was and returned with Isabelle. She slogged in, her eyes hidden behind big, dark, round sunglasses. Luca had to guide her down the hall from the front door. Though as she turned the corner, Isabelle broke free of him and felt for the nearest wall. She read it like Braille until she reached the living room.

"Good morning," she managed in a low, muffled tone. She slumped onto Luca's sofa, reclining in a way that made her appear more of a puddle than a person.

Determined to finish the conversation they'd started, Luca asked Ansel to head outside with him. "Issy, we're stepping out for a quick toke," Luca said.

"Go ahead, don't mind me. I need to catch up on my beauty rest."

Luca motioned to Ansel, and they exited the kitchen through its heavy glass sliding door. "Only Issy would come over and take a nap," he said. Ansel laughed and nodded in agreement. As soon as they stepped outside, Luca dipped into his pocket and retrieved a perfectly rolled joint which he handed to Ansel for inspection.

"Beautiful. Is this your work?"

"Handcrafted."

"The true cure for hangovers." Luca slipped a lighter out of his pocket and handed it to Ansel. Ansel smelled the sweet aroma emanating from the joint as he lit it. He stepped off Luca's backdoor patio and sunk his bare feet into the dewy grass of the backyard. Most of the yard was grass, neatly trimmed, with mixed gravel lining the perimeter.

"So, what are you going to do?"

Ansel inhaled deeply, exhaled a thick white cumulus cloud of smoke. "About?" He had hoped against his better judgment that if he successfully played ignorant, the problem would somehow evaporate.

"You know what I'm talking about." Luca was cool yet stern.

Ansel took another puff, blew the smoke out in big rings. "I don't know. What can I do? I certainly can't tell my mom that I've dropped out and started selling dope to my old classmates."

"Does weed count as dope?" Luca asked, taking the joint from Ansel. He took a hit and paused. He stood perfectly still, holding the joint in one hand, musing, eyes fixed toward the sky. He exhaled and took another hit before passing the joint back to Ansel.

"It all counts as dope." Ansel inhaled once this time and let the smoke ease its way out through his nostrils. He returned the joint to Luca.

"Okay, maybe leave out the part about selling illicit drugs." Luca took another big puff of the joint himself, then another and offered it back to Ansel, who waved it off politely.

"I'd still have to explain what I did with my tuition money for last year."

Luca finished smoking. He snuffed the joint out gently using the tips of his fingers. "True. I guess there's no way to untangle that web, huh?"

"Nope. I mean I missed you guys, you and Isabelle, but honestly, I don't think I can stay here. I love my life in Philly. If we were to sell the house, I could stop dealing. I'd have enough to get by, until I figure out what else I want to do."

"Can't you stop dealing now, live off of what your mom gives you?"

"I did the math; it's not enough." The cool morning air nipped at Ansel's legs as he said this. He shivered slightly. He took another puff of the joint and leaned up against the sliding door. Luca leaned back with him. The sky was a milky blur, sunlight straining to break through the morning clouds. Ansel blinked. His eyelids felt heavy. His mind drifted away, until he wasn't in Hunter any longer. He was in Philadelphia. and it was autumn. All the leaves on the trees that lined the roads had turned a dazzling saffron.

Pedestrians huddled in coats, gloves, and scarves, while bicyclists braved the cold in lycra suits. Cars honked, impatient, late for work, school, and God knows where else. It was bustling, yet humble. It was scenic and vibrant, and Ansel loved it all. It was his first time away from home, save of course for an occasional tension-filled family vacation. He recalled his first taste of Philadelphia air and how exhilarating it had been to taste the air somewhere different after nineteen years of the same-old, same-old. After his second year in the wonderful, cultural

Mecca that is Philly, he had grown tired of having to cut down on his discovery time for class.

When he wasn't in class, he was on the train to New York City with Holly. He was pissing in the dark, drunk in Times Square, currents of fear and laughter running through him concurrently. He was holding Holly back from punching men who catcalled her. He was on the subway kissing some tattooed nerdy dude he'd just met at a bookstore. He was in the car on the way to Jersey, dancing along to the Cure. As all good disasters have, it started out as a joke. He was nineteen.

It was the summer after he completed his sophomore year at Walden. He returned to Hunter but didn't tell his family until after he had been back for four days. Instead of going home, he alternated between staying with Luca and Isabelle. One night while at a pool hall, Ansel made friends with a guy named Trevor. At first, Ansel had been flirting with Trevor, but as the conversation progressed it became obvious Trevor was straight. Still, he wasn't overly macho. He didn't feel the need to shy away from engaging in harmless minor intimacies like touching another guy's shoulder. He and Ansel hit it off so well that Trevor ended up inviting Ansel and his friends to a party at his place in Riverton.

Riverton was a neighboring town, directly north of Hunter. It was known for two things: being the mail processing center of the county and its underground drug capital. Intrigued by its reputation for the latter, Ansel, Luca, and Isabelle set off for the party. They were greeted by a guest on MDMA and spent fifteen minutes talking to a couple who claimed to have shared the best coke ever. They wound up having a discussion and decided to maybe try one drug altogether. They worked their way through the crowd and approached Trevor together. They wound up sharing a joint until the others casually wandered off in their own different directions, leaving Ansel alone with Trevor.

The boys spoke more, and Ansel mentioned he was going to school in Philly, which prompted Trevor to mention a connection he had there. He referred to him as "a comrade in the tireless fight to keep society green." Ansel picked up on the joke right away, and they both laughed heartily. Once the laughter settled, Trevor broke back into serious tones.

"He moved to upstate New York. Haven't been able to find a replacement in the metro area since." Trevor glanced at Ansel. It was only momentarily, but he made sure to make direct eye to eye contact, as if he was sending a signal. "You know..." he said, before cutting himself off abruptly. "Never mind."

Ansel's eyes practically lit up. Partially due to the danger, the excitement of it all, but also the result of something much deeper. He felt the chance to quench a nagging desire, the omnipresent need to be selected, to feel wanted, chosen. Yet, he couldn't give it all away. He couldn't appear too eager. "What?" Ansel asked, half curious, half already knowing what might come next.

"Nothing," Trevor said, "not sure it's a good idea." But that was bullshit. Ansel would later learn that Trevor was merely playing hard to get. He had watched Ansel at the pool hall, picked him out. He knew from the first time they spoke that Ansel would make a good dealer. That's why he invited Ansel to the party. This was a test.

"Well, all right." Ansel was absolutely entranced at this point but determined not to let it show. Little did he know, he'd passed the test.

"Wait," Trevor said. He placed his hand on Ansel's shoulder and pulled Ansel in close. "I was gonna say, if you want to make some good money, you should let me know."

Ansel deliberated. If he sold enough, he'd be able to gain financial independence from his mother. He could maybe stop going to his boring-ass classes, and actually get out there and photograph the world. He could reconsider whether photography was something he cared to do in the first place. He also had run into quite a bit of debt after his freshman year. Things were more expensive in Philly than they were in Hunter, and no one had ever taught him how to manage his money.

"Just weed?"

"Weed, X, white girl, I have a hand in a little of everything, but look, I'll only give you what you think you can move." Trevor's hand rose across his head in a mock salute. Unlike California, where cannabis was legalized for medical purposes, there was no easy way to score it in Philly. *And who doesn't love ecstasy? These are relatively harmless drugs. They'll practically sell themselves.* There was a market and he had solid reasons. Solid enough to him anyway. His friends went home from the party that night, raving about how it had changed them. The next day, Ansel told Luca what happened.

"We leave you alone for half an hour, and you become a drug dealer," Luca had said, laughing a bit, trying to hide the deep well of concern that was bubbling up behind his eyes.

"I'm only going to sell pot and ecstasy." Ansel had a sense of surety that shocked even himself. Whether Ansel was as confident as he sounded or not, Luca was assuaged enough to agree to take him back up to Riverton. With three days left of his trip, they were speeding up Townsend Road in Luca's car to everyone's local haven of sin. Next thing they knew, they were standing on a street named Folsom Lane. Ansel hadn't remembered how small and quaint the street was until then . Neither of them could find the address using the GPS built into their phones. Eventually, Luca went on memory alone.

Despite having been there once before, they were both surprised what a nice neighborhood it was. After all, they had only ever been at night. In the light of day, they could see the streets were well-kept, cars parked on both sides—mostly sedans and family vehicles. The lawns were all well-manicured with neatly trimmed hedges. It wasn't the sea of broken bottles and hypodermic needles you'd expect to find in a place with the reputation that Riverton has. They walked up to Trevor's apartment building. It stood glistening in the sun, far shinier and newer than the neighboring buildings. Large glass windows framed the entire lobby. They used the intercom this time, something Ansel had not remembered them doing the night of the party. Trevor answered and buzzed them up.

They walked up to an elevator and exited on the fourth floor. Trevor was pleasant. He'd been twenty-one at the time, which was two years older than Ansel and Luca. Trevor met Luca at the Catholic Church their families both forced them to go to. There were no weapons lying around, no drugs, and no junkies. His apartment was almost as immaculate as Isabelle's. Trevor made small talk, but he was charismatic. He shared that his parents were divorced. When asked where they were, he told them that his mom was on vacation in Gibraltar, and his dad was probably off having another kid.

They enjoyed each other's presence for a moment until Ansel brought the conversation around to why they were meeting. Trevor told Ansel his uncle and cousin ran a dispensary in town. They had a driver in Newark, who would make trips to the Pennsylvania border to drop off the goods. All Ansel would have to do is drive to meet him twice a week: once to receive a shipment and once to exchange cash. The shipments would start at three ounces; if Ansel was able to sell out fast enough, it would increase to six. Ansel went back to Philly, and two weeks later, he was sitting on the banks of Cresheim Creek in Fairmount Park.

He was with Holly and two of his sociology classmates. The four of them sat out on a picnic blanket. His classmates were test subjects. They bought an eighth of a gram each, and Ansel had paid himself for two eighths as well (so that he and Holly could smoke with them). They danced on the banks, and one of the classmates fell into the creek. Holly climbed a tree and began meditating. It was wondrous. Each classmate told two of their other classmates, who in turn told two more people, and by the end of the week, Ansel had sold out. He called Trevor from Philly and told him his friends there loved the product. Nothing was ever the same after that.

"Ansel!" Luca's voice brought Ansel back into the present moment. It was deep yet sharp and cut the air crisp off of Ansel's reveries on that quiet morning.

"Sorry, man, I drifted off."

"It's cool. You're making excuses." Luca brought them right back to the topic at hand. What was Ansel going to do? He could not keep up the charade forever. He was going to have to admit that he'd dropped out. Either that, or he was going to have to graduate from Walden.

Ansel knew even if they sold the house and he deferred a year or so at Walden, he could not live off the funds forever. His job at Artist Etc. was fine, but he didn't earn nearly enough to pay his rent. He didn't live in a fancy apartment either. It was minimalistic, and not by any accounts lavish. He was equipped with mostly the essentials. He was mindful about paying his bills on time, and he tried to live as frugally as possible. But he overspent by a lot after his first year.

After wanting nothing but distance from his family for as long as he could remember, he finally had it and he couldn't survive without them. It was a terrible case of irony. He dreaded that he would always be a part of the dysfunctional unit. Despite the constant bickering and the lies, they weren't bad people. The problem was that stuff—his father's slew of lovers, the bickering, and the lies—that stuff sticks to you like tar. You try to scrape it off until your fingertips are raw, only to discover it is set in, tattooed forever. "You're right. The truth is I know I will have to tell them about school eventually. I'm not ready yet." Luca nodded, knowing the decision had been made.

Chapter Five

Regina strutted through the upstairs hall like the queen of the manor, although she couldn't stop the walls from whispering years of history to her. They reminded her of her youth. She saw herself as a small child, hiding, laughing, and running through the halls during a game of tag with her siblings. She saw herself standing at the top of the staircase plotting, eager to catch them. She wasn't a small child anymore.

She was fourteen and walking down those same stairs for her first day in high school. Her hair was down, wild, and resting at her shoulders. Her style had evolved with her sense of self. She was coming into her own. She had been hailed by the art world for her talent for almost a decade, and she had finally begun to understand what that meant.

She eased past the stairs, and as she approached Elise's room, she was fifteen now and had lived at home for a year without her sister. She missed Elise. Regina had made friends at school, but it wasn't the same. She longed for more than the world she was living in. She longed for adventure, crowded cafés, and freezing New York City air. She did her research and presented her mother with a plan.

She would join her sister in New York and finish school, all under the watchful eye of their mother's older sister, Aunt Nell. She recalled the feeling of stepping off the plane in a whole new city, a new world. Time had raced by since then. Regina didn't need anyone's permission to do anything or go anywhere now. She walked up to her brother's childhood bedroom and knocked firmly on the door. When she did not hear a response, she knocked again, this time setting off a loud thud on one of the well-built, double doors leading into the bedroom. She knocked a third time, adding, "Ansel, are you there?"

When she still received no response to her inquiry, Regina turned one of the handles and opened the door wide. She discovered the room was vacant, her little brother nowhere in sight. She left the room and strode back down the hall to her own. Once inside, she waltzed over to her bed. She lay down, picked up her phone from the nightstand, and typed out a text message to her brother.

Chapter Six

Ansel and Luca made their way back into the house from the backyard. A wad of loose blades of grass stuck to Ansel's shoes, and he hurriedly wiped them clean on the outdoor mat. The boys strolled into the living room to find Isabelle tucked up on the couch with a thin blanket. She was watching a comedy special.

"Well, remember I had her first," Isabelle said seemingly out of nowhere.

"What?" the boys both answered almost in unison.

"Ally Beckman. We hooked up once during summer camp, right before seventh grade," she clarified, smiling slyly. "Sorry, Ansel, beat you to it."

Ansel laughed. "Thanks for the heads up, but we're friends." He sat down beside her and noticed he'd received a text. Ansel pulled his phone from his pocket and saw the message was from Regina. He opened it begrudgingly. It read:

It's time to talk decisions. Meet me in an hour at our favorite coffee shop downtown.

The lack of details, other than the fundamental ones, did not frighten Ansel. If this had been before he had moved to Philly, it might have. He might have read the tone and realized that she was being ominous on purpose. *Typical Regina.* Though he wasn't afraid, he did feel something in the pit of his stomach. It was a dull, nauseating feeling. He knew whatever she wanted to talk about would not be pleasant. He inhaled, the air of the room filling his lungs, sweeping out with a steady exhale.

Luca walked over to him and put his hands on Ansel's shoulders in an effort to calm him down. He began massaging.

"I've gotta go meet Regina."

Almost instinctively, Luca replied with one word, "Godspeed," and he finished up the shoulder message and released his friend.

Feeling a bit more relaxed, Ansel thanked Luca and headed inside. He gathered some clothes and went straight into Luca's guest bathroom. He showered and shaved away the shadow that had taken over his face since he'd left Philadelphia. He was to meet Regina at her favorite coffee shop, which conveniently was only about eight blocks away from Luca's house. The trip would take fifteen minutes or less on foot. He peered at himself in the large single mirror that covered most of the bathroom wall it hung on. If he was perfectly honest, he had to admit he had grown tired of lying. He was tired of the façade he had to paint for his family.

He was tired of keeping his story afloat. It had become a full-time job. When he first started at Walden College, his parents bought him an ultra-expensive camera. This was no big deal at first, since he was actually attending classes. However, once he stopped, he knew he had to either come clean or keep up appearances. The former did not feel like it was a viable option at the time, so Ansel opted for the latter. He took a million and one photos with that ultra-expensive camera.

He disguised the good ones as projects and sent the occasional copy to his mother. He fabricated tales about quirky professors (mostly from accounts shared with him by peers). He staged stress over midterms. Every detail of his waking life was contrived with painstaking effort. All for what? Between his sisters falling out and his grand-dad's health deteriorating, his mother had probably hardly had time to notice, let alone examine the details of his college life.

The more he thought about it, the more he realized he could've come clean to his mother months ago. There would have probably been little to no penalty at all. Yet, despite it all he didn't tell her It didn't even occur to him to tell her or anyone else in his family. He was too worried that he would disappoint them. He was mired in the fear and self-doubt. He was afraid of being the talentless Wallis child, the one who failed at getting a higher education—failed at everything.

Failure was not an option for a Wallis. He knew that all too well. He decided it was better that he kept his mouth shut about quitting school. The same way he had kept his mouth shut about running out of money after his freshman year. He assumed the loan he borrowed would solve his problems. He had told himself that he would be fine. *I'll catch up, get out of the red, and I'll pay it off.* But another year went by, and he never quite caught up.

His mother would send him some money, if he asked, but it always came with strings. He absolutely abhorred that, so he stopped asking. He came home after his soph-omore year, deeper into debt than he had ever thought he could be. Selling cannabis presented an easy solution, and before long he got into selling ecstasy as well. He continued accepting his mom's money for tuition but didn't ask for anything else. She didn't investigate, and he stayed silent.

He wasn't sure what Regina was planning. As he stepped into the shower, he was sure of one thing: he was not afraid. The water felt cool and cleansing upon his head. Eight blocks and forty-five minutes later, he was face-to-face with his older sister at Russo's Café. She'd chosen a table on the patio, under one of the many giant beige umbrellas. Their umbrella swayed with the summer breeze, and Regina's closely cropped dark hair followed suit. As soon as Ansel sat, Regina pulled out a cigarette and casually offered him one. This time he turned her down, sensing the arrival of his impending doom.

"Let's talk negotiations," she started. She had already ordered a Bloody Mary and began sipping it slow and sinister. "I know you haven't been going to school for the last year. I know you don't want Mom to find out, and I'm willing to keep it to myself, so long as you agree to sell the house."

"That's not a negotiation, that's called blackmail."

"Call it what you want. I've got you by the stones, and I want to get rid of the house."

A server walked over, so Ansel muted himself. She was tall and pretty with big brown eyes that stood out against her lily-white uniform shirt and apron. She asked if they needed anything, and with a feigned air of relaxation, Ansel ordered a double shot of vodka. As the server vanished into the bar, the heated conversation resumed. "And if I don't agree?" Ansel said. He was projecting courage now, seated upright and staring his sister directly in the eyes. He had decided he would not back down so easily.

"If you don't agree, I tell Mom everything. She'll cut off your monthly cash flow, and you'll have to move back to this miserable little one-horse town."

"Did anyone ever tell you you're a truly awful person?"

"Look, I hate to do this, but you know me. I'm like a piece by Kruger."

"You are not what you seem?"

"I was thinking more complex, torn in my different directions. Right now, I'm torn about ratting on my little brother." The arrogance of her speech flowed through the air on the same wavelength of diplomats and royals. She was Pharaoh and the art world was her Egypt. She had conquered and ruled with stunning piece after stunning piece. A new light installation here, an innovative sculpture there. She won awards, traveled Europe, and even got married.

"I had some papers drawn up. Read them over. Our profits would be insane. It is definitely a seller's market," Regina said.

"Have you stopped to consider that we'll lose a piece of our family history?"

"History doesn't live in a single place; it travels with you."

He hated how stoic she was sometimes. He browsed over the paperwork. She was right. Yet, as much as he wanted to get away from Hunter, as much as he could use the money, he couldn't bring himself to agree.

"I don't expect an answer tonight. I know you've only been here a few days. Take a week or so to think it over and get back to me." She slid the paperwork over to him.

He stared at the papers for a minute, picked them up. He folded them in all together, neatly into fourths, and placed them in his back pocket.

"One week!"

As he got up to leave, the server reappeared with the double shot he'd ordered. Ansel drank it in full within seconds. "Rot in hell," he said to his sister before he walked away.

On the way back to Luca's house, Ansel began craving a cigarette and another drink. He stopped off at a convenience store to satisfy this desire. The store was lit by faint fluorescent bulbs and the floors heavily scuffed. Situated a few feet from the entrance was a large, low countertop with a clerk behind it, who was busy reading some heavy novel. Ansel shuffled to the walk-in freezer at the back of the store. He grabbed a six-pack of pilsners and purchased it along with a pack of Marlboro Lights and a lighter. The clerk completed the entire transaction without looking up from her book.

Once outside, Ansel withdrew a single cigarette, slipped the pack back into the little plastic bag that the store clerk had given him. He lit the cigarette with his free hand. The bottles in the bag clinked together as he walked the rest of the way to Luca's.

"You got beer. What happened"" He welcomed Ansel inside.

"Regina knows everything somehow, and she's black-mailing me."

"What do you mean, she knows *everything*?"

Holly and Luca were the only people who knew Ansel wasn't going to school. Holly was not the kind of person to betray a secret, and neither was Luca, for that matter. Holly had found out early on. Ansel had been sloppy. He'd confessed to Luca, because he had to tell someone, and Luca was the least judgmental of his group of friends. That's why it didn't make any sense. *Regina must've found out another way, but how?*

Paranoia completely engulfed Ansel. He racked his brain, wondering how his sister managed to find out that he'd dropped out. Did she have some kind of informant working at his school? A friend at the admissions office perhaps? Did she hire a private investigator? No, that would be extreme, even for her. Ansel stared out of the glass sliding door that led out to the backyard, while all of these thoughts ran through his head.

"You look like you need some air."

Ansel did not answer. *How could Regina have known?* he thought, still wrestling with the improbability of it all.

Having noticed the lack of a response from his friend, Luca decided to take control of the situation. "Let's all step out into the backyard again." He grabbed Ansel by the hand and led him outside. Ansel moved forward but failed to speak.

It doesn't make any sense, he thought. *Someone had to have betrayed me. It couldn't have been Holly, or Luca, but how? And she's blackmailing me. This is my sister. This is my life.* They'd reached the sliding door, and as Luca went to open it, Ansel fell dizzily to the floor. He awoke sprawled out on the sofa to a slow pitter-patter coming from outside. It had begun to rain. As he sat up, Ansel felt a sharp vibration from inside his pocket. Once again it was a text, this time from his sister Elise.

The message read: *Your presence is requested at the house tonight for dinner.*

"Just when you think it can't get any worse," he said aloud. He dressed in slim denim jeans, a navy T-shirt, a black blazer, and brown leather oxfords. He brushed his hands through his hair, put on cologne, and was prepared for battle. "Luca, if you would please drive me to my mom's house, I would appreciate it."

"Are you certain?" Luca asked.

"Yes," Ansel answered, "and yes, Isabelle, you can come."

"I was going to anyway," Isabelle said charmingly.

The rain picked up as they headed down the hall to the elevator. It was absolutely pouring by the time the elevator door opened. Ansel and Luca walked in after Isabelle. Luca immediately stood in front of the door facing them. "Wouldn't be odd if someone did this?" he asked. "Why hasn't anyone done this?"

Ansel couldn't contain himself and began laughing first. Isabelle followed suit. Luca began laughing. After a few minutes, the doors opened once more.

"We were lucky no one got on. They would've thought we were insane," Isabelle said.

"Aren't we?" Ansel asked.

Luca pressed the little key on the car remote. A loud beeping and a flash of light reverberated throughout the otherwise dim parking garage beneath the building. Luca unlocked the doors to his car. They piled in. Ansel shut his eyes, and Valse De Virgine played. His fingers swayed with the music. They drove away from the glittering city lights, bidding them farewell, as the road grew steeper and darker. It took them thirty-five minutes to arrive at the old colonial. Ansel waved goodbye to his friends and strode up to the front door, still big, black, imposing. The rain had let up for a bit. He used the knocker to knock three solid times, and Elise came to the door.

"Glad you could make it."

The ease with which she said this relaxed Ansel a bit. Elise's presence in general eased him. Regina had a flare for the dramatic, *a family trait*, so he was unsure whether to expect a showdown or their typical frigid dinner for four. He followed Elise across the foyer and into the living room. They stood before the dark oak double doors, its stained-glass windows glinting in the light that ventured in from the other side of the room. Ansel twisted the doorknob, eager to get this all over with. He and Elise walked inside, and she shut the doors behind them.

Regina and their mother were already seated. Elise sat down directly across from Regina and Ansel sat opposite their mother. He pulled his chair out from under the table with a rattle. It was a glass dining table with capacity for six, held up by sturdy wooden legs that climbed beneath it like tree branches. Of course, one big branch stood solitary in the middle for added support. The Wallises all sat around the table for a moment, face-to-face.

Steam wafted into the air from the food. Their mother encouraged them to serve themselves. Regina served herself first, adding cucumber salad and a giant scoop of brown rice onto her plate. Ansel grabbed some spinach and Elise went for the salt fish. All four of the Wallises continued like this, applying various portions to their plates for several minutes. There was a subtle calm that had taken over the room as they did, the kind of harmony that only comes with a shared meal. Hunger works in strange ways.

The hot food awaiting them somehow made them more civil to one another. They passed dishes back and forth politely. This was the only time that they had all been genuinely polite to one another in ages. Sadly, once the first bite was taken, the harmony dissipated. They were brought back down from whatever cloud they had momentarily visited. Back down to reality they sunk, as Regina announced she was certain they would be rid of the house soon.

"Granddad purchased this house for us. When he did, the thought of a black man owning property in this neighborhood, let alone a colonial of all things, was practically unheard of. And you want to throw that all away," Elise said.

"Pretty much," Regina replied flatly.

"Well, don't be so sure you'll succeed. It's up to Ansel now," Elise said. She took a bite of her salt fish and rice.

With that, Regina would have normally been silenced, but she had more ammo in her arsenal this time. She had a secret weapon. Ansel wasn't in school. "Well, yes. That aside, I've had a talk with Ansel, and I'm pretty certain he wants to sell the house, too, which would mean the house goes."

Elise dropped her spoon onto her dinner plate. The thud it made echoed throughout the room. "Ansel, is this true, have you come to a decision?" she asked. Her voice was heavy with disappointment, as if they had had some agreement that she would be the first one to know what he decided to do.

"Um, well, I," Ansel stammered. His tongue became cold, hard and thick, as though it were freezing over in his mouth. He interlocked his fingers, nervously kneading his thumbs together.

"Ansel, remember what we talked about," Regina said, her words quick and hot. She was threatening him, warning him to toe the line, reminding him of the leverage she held over him.

"Ansel, think for yourself, don't let Regina sway you," Elise added.

Ansel felt as though he were stuck in one of those scenes, those TV/movie tropes where there's an angel whispering advice on one shoulder and a little devil doing the same on the other. It was nauseating. It made his head spin.

"Oh, shut the hell up," Regina said to Elise.

"You shut the hell up," Elise said with equal conviction. "What do you mean 'remember what you talked about'? Are you trying to bribe or blackmail him or something?"

"What?" Regina said, employing her best impression of outrage. She gathered her napkin from her lap and thrust it onto the table for added effect.

"He hasn't even been here for a week, and indecision plagued him when we last spoke," Elise said. She threw her napkin on the table as well, crossed her arms, and glared at straight at Regina.

"I was, I am, I..." Ansel started, this time trying to add a bit more force to his voice as he spoke. Unfortunately, before he could finish, Regina chimed in again.

"Ansel wants to sell the house. In fact, he's here to deliver some documents that he signed stating so," she said confidently. She, too, crossed her arms and glared back at her sister.

"I can speak for myself," Ansel shouted, throwing his hands into the air.

The whole room went quiet. Mrs. Wallis spoke, "So speak, son. What is it that you want to do with the house?"

"I want to know why you want to sell it for one," Ansel said to his mother.

"Simply put, I, like Regina, have grown tired of this house," Mrs. Wallis said. "To be perfectly honest, I hated it from the moment your granddad bought it. But I understood what it meant to him, and I figured I could grow to love it. While I've had good memories here, unfortunately it doesn't outweigh the bad. Since you kids live elsewhere, and your father and grandfather have both now passed, I see no reason to keep it."

"And I think that Mom should let me buy her out," Elise said. "You, me, and Regina will be the ones passing this place down to the next generation anyway."

"Ansel, honey," his mother said, staring him directly in the eyes, "why don't you tell us, in your own words, what would you like to do?"

"I don't know," Ansel said, strangely overcome with the inability to lie. He took a breath and noticed how tense his neck and shoulders had grown.

"Ansel hasn't been going to school for the last year," Regina blurted out.

"I already knew that," Mrs. Wallis said swiftly. She idly tapped her fingernails on the dinner table. She so was calm and collected.

"What?" Ansel asked, genuinely bewildered. He watched as Regina slunk down in her chair, defeated. The smug expression on her face dissolved. Her cocky demeanor shifted to one of sheer agitation and dismay. It sent a small wave of joy through him to see misery consume her, but he did his best to hide it. It wasn't time to gloat yet, not until he knew more about how his mother found out that he wasn't in school.

"I've known for about the past six months." Mrs. Wallis said. "I hope you at least did something valuable with the tuition money your grandfather and I gave you. You could've put on a small production of that play you were writing. What was it called, 'The Disintegration'?"

"No, Mom, I believe it was called 'The Desolate,'" Elise said.

"Actually, 'The Deserted,'" Ansel said, huffing under his breath.

"Well, whatever it's titled, you could have completed it by now. That or you could have added a decent blazer to your wardrobe." his mother added, pointing at his outfit.

Ansel rolled his eyes. He knew his mother must have been telling the truth; she must've known for a while. Otherwise, she would have been outraged, red-faced, shouting at him for wasting her hard-earned money. "If you already knew that I dropped out, why didn't you say anything sooner?"

"Honestly, I am waiting for you to come to me," Mrs. Wallis said.

Ansel couldn't help but follow up with another question. "How did you find out?" he asked. He had to know. Between Regina miraculously finding out and his secret, Ansel was certain he had someone in his inner circle that he couldn't truly trust, but he wasn't sure whom. Holly, Luca, Isabelle—none of them had any motive to do this.

"Your friend Sebastian told me," Mrs. Wallis said plainly.

The rain pelted down harder and harder outside. The ferocity of it reminded Ansel of the end of Sebastian's visit to Philly. Sebastian had stayed with him for two weeks, the entirety of spring break. The weather had gone through its usual fluctuations, bright and sunny one moment, light showers the next, but the day Sebastian left was different. It rained heavily for most of the day. Ansel had been extra careful during those two weeks to conceal his double life, or so he thought.

He got up at different hours of the day, to pretend to go to class. Most of the time, he would find a park to get stoned and meditate in. He'd sell to a few students and go off to Lorenzo's on Twenty-Fifth Street for a slice of pizza. *How did Sebastian find out I wasn't in school any longer?* Ansel thought. *Why on earth did he tell my mom?* These were questions that Ansel assumed were going to have to wait until after dinner to be answered, but he was wrong.

"Don't be too hard on him. I suppose my telling him how worried I was about you did the trick. And I do miss you. You don't really communicate with me."

"I write or call you at least twice a month," Ansel said. And he did reach out to her at least twice a month, on Sundays. It had been one of the few rituals he had developed and stuck to, to keep up the ruse that he was still attending classes.

"Sure, you write and you call, but you always say that you're fine. I needed to know what was really going on. I hardly know anything about you. Are you seeing any nice boys or girls?"

"I don't want to talk about it, Mom."

"You never want to talk about it. You know I've already accepted your lifestyle choice."

"My lifestyle choice, what does that even mean? I'm bisexual; it's not like I've gone off to live on a commune."

"The point is that I don't care whom you sleep with. It is my job to nurture you. It is a pity you're giving up, since you were one of the few black students at Walden, but I realize that college isn't for everyone. I expect you to pay me back for the tuition I spent this past year," she said. "But I understand. I need you to be honest with me."

While he couldn't entirely disagree with what his mother had to say, the last part of her speech was especially patronizing to him. "Forgive me, but you are one of the most dishonest people I know," he said. "You just admitted to manipulating one of my best friends in order to get information on me."

"Well, what other choice did I have?" Mrs. Wallis asked calmly.

"I don't know, but maybe you could have chosen not to enlist one of my closest friends to betray me," Ansel said.

"Be that as it may, it doesn't change the fact that I'm your parent," Mrs. Wallis interrupted. "I love you, and I want to set you on the right path, Ansel."

"Since when? When have you ever paid attention to me? I tried to kill myself, and all you did was complain about having to replace the tile because there was much too much blood soaked into the grout and the subfloor."

"Ansel, that's not fair," Elise said in their mother's defense. "That was a tough time for all of us, especially Mom."

"Well, things are heating up now," Regina said with a sly smile on her face. She swirled her wine glass round and round.

"Damn it, Regina, can you please stop being a bitch for a single minute?" Elise said. She clenched both of her fists and slammed them down on the table.

"I could, but where's the fun in that?" Regina replied.

"You know what kills me?" Ansel said frankly, turning toward each of his sisters. "I still don't know why you two aren't speaking."

"You two aren't speaking? Since when?" Mrs. Wallis asked, her voice laden with concern.

"It's been a year and a half," Regina said.

"Why is it you two aren't speaking anymore?" Ansel asked. He looked to Regina, but he could tell she had no intention of providing an explanation.

"I, personally, would love to know," Mrs. Wallis added. Sensing, as Ansel did, that Regina was not the party that would divulge the truth, she turned to face Elise.

Elise could tell her mother and brother weren't going to back down. Meanwhile Regina sat ever so smugly across from her, almost daring her to say something. She had had enough. Elise inhaled deeply. "We aren't speaking because Regina fucked the artistic director of my dance consortium, which, of course, resulted in fucking me out of a job," she said through gritted teeth.

"Elise, honey, language."

"Oh God, for the millionth time, it just happened. You make it sound like I was out to seduce him. Besides, the real reason you're upset isn't because your boss threw a tantrum and you lost out on dancing in some show. It's because you're jealous. You wanted him, and you're jealous that he wanted me. Admit it!" Regina said.

"Do you hear yourself right now? You sound like a complete narcissist," Elise said.

"I have to get the hell out of here," Ansel muttered to himself. He cleared his throat to interrupt the chaotic round table. "You know what, Regina is right. I want to sell. I'm selling my share of the house to Elise."

Regina looked like she had lost all hope for oxygen. And like that, Ansel had broken free, free of his family, free of their expectations, free to finally do as he pleased.

Chapter Seven

Ansel invited Sebastian to the house via text message. *I've missed you, come over?* Sebastian hastily agreed. He must have sped down the road from his family's house to Ansel's, because he was there in record time.

"Hey," Sebastian said, cute and casual at the front door. Ansel led Sebastian into the foyer and up the stairs to his room. He turned the knob, and Sebastian flushed to the cheeks and finally broke his silence. "This is erotic. I love mystery."

By then they were safely inside Ansel's room. Ansel looked Sebastian deep in the eyes and said, "I know you told my mom that I dropped out of school. How did you know?"

"I'm sorry," Sebastian said shaking from nervousness. Ansel couldn't ever remember seeing him lose his cool before.

"How did you know?" Ansel was determined to appear unfazed by the change in Sebastian's temperament.

"You told me." Sebastian stepped back a bit. He sighed and sat down on Ansel's bed. Ansel noticed Sebastian tuck his hands together in an effort to control their trembling.

"No, I didn't."

"Oh, but you did," Sebastian rose to stand. "I overheard you and Holly talking during my visit to Philly. You were all 'I never dreamed I would drop out but here I am.' I thought it was hysterical at first, and I heard Holly's reaction and realized it wasn't a joke. I waited for you to tell me, but you never did." He walked over to the bedroom window and leaned on the sill. Everything in him wanted to climb out of it and run off. Yet he also wanted to stay, needed it, because he needed Ansel's forgiveness.

Ansel furrowed his brows. He crossed his arms and gritted his teeth in anger but did not raise his voice. "So, you decided from there to go and tell my mom?" He walked over to the window as well and stared Sebastian straight in the eyes.

Sebastian looked down at the floor, looked up at Ansel. "You know me better than that," he said, his grey eyes filled with sadness. "She made me promise."

"What?"

"When I got back from Philly, your mom sorta summoned me. She said she got my number from my mom, and that she wanted to make sure you were doing all right. She said you always sent her bland letters. It sounded like you were going to school and getting along, but she couldn't tell. She couldn't tell anything from your social media accounts either. She wanted to know how you were living, and that you were happy."

"She used you, Sebastian. She manipulated you into feeding her info on me. She practically admitted it at dinner."

"Well, at the time it sounded like a concerned mom who wanted to know her son was all right. I started out lying for you, but she asked too many follow-up questions. I didn't know what to do, so I told her that you dropped out."

Ansel could tell from the look in Sebastian's eyes that he was being honest. He paced away from Sebastian.

"Whether I overheard you or not I was bound to figure it out. I stayed with you for two weeks. I'm your best friend, or at least I used to be. I know you. You left like three or four times during those few weeks. You made up some dumb excuse each time and went to handle whatever it was that you had to handle. I figured it had to be drugs, and knowing you, I couldn't imagine any hard stuff."

"I'd tell you, but I feel like you'd run off and tell my mom."

"I told your mom about school because it's important. I care about you, and you were getting yourself into something you couldn't get out of. And yes, maybe I thought they'd make you stick around, and I'd get to see you more, but that was not why I told her."

"Well, your courageous effort was all for naught. I'm going to let Elise buy me out. She, Regina, and our mom can squabble amongst themselves."

Sebastian's jaw had dropped. He wasn't sure what to say, what to do, until he saw Ansel open the bedroom door—a clear indicator that he should leave. Sebastian walked out of the room, down the stairs to the foyer.

Ansel waited at the front door as Sebastian left. They didn't kiss, they didn't embrace, they didn't even say goodbye. Instead, Sebastian got into an olive-green sedan. *Too rainy for the moped,* Ansel thought.

Sebastian sat there for a moment. Ansel wondered if he, too, were fighting back the urge to scream, cry, or curse the very idea of love aloud. It took everything in Ansel not to yell after Sebastian to come back. *But what would that truly accomplish?* he thought to himself. The rain was softened to a drizzle. Ansel and Sebastian looked at each other one last time, knowing neither was going to cave in. Sebastian gave a half-hearted wave as he drove away. All Ansel could do was stand there watching, as he choked back tears.

Ansel called Luca and asked if Luca could pick him up down the road. Ansel walked until he had reached the spot where they had agreed to meet. The entire time, he hummed and drummed his fingers against his thigh. He couldn't help but feel the exuberance of no longer being tied to this town and the past. He could go back to Philly now. He could do whatever he wanted. His mom knew he'd dropped out of school. Regina had no leverage over him. And it truly hit him: he had no reason left to stay until the end of summer.

Ansel knew what he had to do next. He had to go to Riverton, quit dealing, and head back to Philly. Elise had already sent him a text advising that she'd be sending over some paperwork regarding the house. A few signatures and his shares were as good as sold. Funny how a mountain of torment can be undone with a single idea. Why hadn't he thought of it before? He could sell his share to Elise.

The Wallises all came to resent one another in some way. The normal family dysfunction had grown into awful ache that gnawed at them only in one another's presence. They were each free and happy on their own, but together they were incontestably miserable. Ansel fabricated an existence that he even swept his best friends into. He did it to maintain a life away from them. Holly and Luca had to keep a secret. Isabelle, his mom, his sisters were all kept out of the loop.

He was vague to Ally, vague to everyone unless they asked, and he had to lie. It was such a relief to be able to break out of that. He went into the upstairs bathroom to wash his face. He opened the medicine cabinet, in search of aspirin to ease his oncoming headache. A little container filled with sewing needles fell out. He pricked his finger on one while placing them back into the container. A drop of blood fell into the clean porcelain sink.

In that moment, Ansel was twelve again and staring into the sink as he made up his mind that everything was meaningless. He was meaningless. He had ruined his mother's life, like he ruined everything else all the time. Ansel grew dizzy. It had been a long time since he'd thought of that fateful day. It was an acute reminder of why he couldn't stand to live in the old colonial. Luca picked him up a little while later. As he got in the cruiser and Luca revved the engine, Ansel threw his left hand in the air and flipped his middle finger high. Paperwork, Riverton, and he was home free.

Chapter Eight

Regina sat across from her mother and elder sister.

"Regina, I can't believe that you blackmailed your brother," Mrs. Wallis said, "and, Elise, I still don't like the language you used."

"Is that how we're starting this?" Elise asked.

"Typical Elise, never satisfied," Regina said.

"Shut up, Regina," Mrs. Wallis said. It was clear she had had enough of the unpleasant discourse. Regina was well aware that her mother thought of herself a rather simple woman, even though she was anything but. She enjoyed music, talk of her former career as a dancer, talk of her children's accomplishments, cooking, and solving scientific algorithms in her spare time. She disliked disobedient children and dirt. Any one of her children could easily recall her overreaction to a mess. Regina had a vivid memory of one afternoon where she, Elise, and Ansel were gathered in the living room, where Mrs. Wallis sat them down and asked quite seriously why they hated her. When Elise objected, Mrs. Wallis followed up with, "Well, if you didn't hate me, this house would be clean."

The fact was they didn't hate her. They were children who lived in a fairly big house. It was easy to make little messes everywhere and forget. Mrs. Wallis refused to hire a housekeeper, because despite living in a colonial, that was too pretentious. The Wallis children learned to clean and clean well. It wasn't simply a matter of cleanliness; it was a matter of respect.

"Regina, what have I done to you to warrant such disrespect?" Mrs. Wallis posed, staring her youngest daughter right in the eyes.

Regina glared at her mother. "Where shall we begin?"

The rain let up, as the Wallises sat around their glass dining table, with their sins laid out next to the brioche.

"Well, Regina, I did my best. It's not my fault that your father impressed poor moral attitudes upon you all, by flaunting his adultery and taking his own life," Mrs. Wallis said. She shook uncontrollably.

Regina drank a large gulp of her wine. "Anyone would have offed themselves to get away from you." Before she knew it, Elise had risen and slapped her right across the face. Regina was stunned. Her cheek stung white hot. She could almost feel the blood vessels swell and the redness sweep across her face. In a sudden motion Regina seized her dinner fork and lunged at Elise, stopping short of her neck.

Mrs. Wallis sat tense and erect. "Drop the fork, Regina," she said in an even tone, but her youngest daughter did not respond. Regina was fuming. She could feel her cheek pulsating. Elise meanwhile remained silent. She simply stared her sister in the eye, as if daring Regina to stab her with the fork. Mrs. Wallis continued gently trying to coax Regina to relinquish the fork for a few moments, but she was only met with more silence.

Finally, Mrs. Wallis lost her patience. "Oh, for chrissakes, quit the theatrics and put down the damn fork now."

With that, Regina unclenched her wrists and her fork fell to the table, making a loud pinging sound. Still locked in a death glare with her sister. Regina uttered, "Next time Mom won't be here to save you," then stormed out of the dining room.

Elise and Mrs. Wallis remained seated silently at the table. The echo of Regina's dinner fork hitting the glass table still rang out in the air. As she walked off, Regina held the offended cheek in soreness and in awe. For the first time she recalled, her sister had rendered her speechless.

Chapter Nine

Two days passed. It was a most unbearably warm Friday afternoon. Ansel was sitting in the passenger seat of Luca's car, and they were speeding down Townsend Road again. The wind rode in through the downturned windows. Ansel closed his eyes at the feel of the breeze. He had filled Luca in on everything, the night of the infamous family dinner, and asked if Luca would drive him up to Riverton. Now that his secret about school was out and he'd had promised his share of the house to Elise, all he had to do was get out of dealing before he went back to Philly.

It was a Friday afternoon, and they were fast approaching the Hunter-Riverton city border. Ansel thought of the drive to the Pennsylvania border. He had listened to music for the first time. Not too loudly, but loud enough to drown out his anxiety. He did not think much of the illegality of cannabis as he used it often. Notwithstanding, moving the stuff across state lines made Ansel acutely aware that he faced arrest if caught. He was almost certain his family would disown him if that happened. "You are not permitted to be a stereotype," Elise would say. Their mother would say something like "Young, black, and in jail is not what we strive for in this family."

Ansel couldn't disagree with them even in his own head, even though they were hypocrites. Yet, he found the rush of risk irresistible. It was probably the first time he'd risked anything in his life. It was due to this hypnotic, romantic rush of adrenaline when he took that risk that Ansel loved being a dope dealer. It was the exchange time that got the best of him the most. The drive was peaceful, and the terms were simple. He was either picking up or dropping off.

When he picked up, he drove down for a shipment. When he dropped off, he was delivering cash from the goods for his cut. The pickups were always on a separate day from the drop-offs, and they were always met with the same routine. Ansel actually got kind of close to Vince, the connection in Jersey. Vince ended up sharing how Trevor's uncle had hired other students. There were two others on the East Coast that Vince knew of, a pre-law student in Florida and a pre-med student in Connecticut. *What distinguished company*, Ansel thought.

They were three students with one thing in common: they all promoted the same product. That made them entrepreneurs in a way. They did receive a cut of the shares after all. For these reasons, Ansel also loved the exchange, right up until the one time when things had gone terribly wrong. That one time, some drunken idiot came at him with a knife. It was his sixth or seventh exchange, so he thought Ansel was a badass. He thought he was invincible.

He stopped off at a bar near the designated meeting place. He had overestimated traffic and arrived ahead of Vince. He thought he would stop off at the bar and have a drink to kill the time. At the bar, a man in the corner nearest to Ansel started shouting his political beliefs. He started spouting hate speech. It only took one time for the "fag" to slip from his mouth before he found Ansel's fist in it. Ansel was not the kind to start fights, but for some reason this man made him absolutely blind with rage. Red, red, all red. Next thing you know Ansel's holding the blade of this guy's knife while kneeing him in the stomach outside.

He wasn't some big trucker guy. Ansel wasn't that crazy. The man was slender and tall, but less fit than Ansel. Ansel also had the advantage when it came to skills. Ansel reduced the man to a pile on the floor and, still clutching the knife, muttered, "Pencil-dick douche." Luckily, Vince kept a first aid kit in his car. He cleaned the wound with iodine and dressed it. Although he warned that Ansel should still see a doctor.

Ansel took his advice. He had stitches put in. It was nothing major, an inch-deep slice in his palm and across a few fingers. He told the doctor he was accosted by a mugger on the street. It was no big deal.

When he broke from his thoughts, they were in Riverton. Luca found parking on Trevor's street. "Are you ready?" he asked.

He had never been more ready and less ready for anything, at the same time. This was not how he imagined things would have gone down. Again, he had not imagined he would ever be in this situation in the first place. He did not feel guilty. He was a supporter of the recreational use of both cannabis and MDMA, always had been. It was the thought that this was a line he hadn't crossed before that made him nervous. Trevor was not violent, so Ansel knew he had nothing to fear from that angle.

There was nothing to be lost. Trevor would find a replacement. Ansel was not holding any product, so there was nothing to exchange. It was a clear cutting of ties. Nothing to fear. No, it was not fear that preoccupied him. It was the dull ache of betrayal. The fact that his best friend had learned his secret and told his mother of all people had set in. His best friend, his lover once. His…he didn't know what.

Not to mention that he still wasn't sure how Regina had found out about the whole affair. There are no secrets in Hunter. There are no places you can go to get away from everyone. You are stranded on an overpopulated isle—what do you bring? Hunter is the suburb television shows are made of. Yes, the ache of betrayal pierced him, but it wasn't solely the betrayal fueling his decision. A burning desire to be free of Hunter, liberated from the cookie-cutter hellhole of a town, coursed through Ansel's veins.

It was also disappointment, massive heavy disappointment riding him, like a child on their father's shoulders. It was this bludgeoning, burdening feeling that he had not only let his mother down, but himself. Oddly enough, though Sebastian hadn't said a word about it, Ansel was plagued with guilt for having kept him in the dark. He couldn't help but wonder what would have happened if he had said something to Sebastian, explained why he'd dropped out, let Sebastian in. Maybe none of this would have happened. He felt terrible for leading a double life.

Ansel and Luca walked toward Trevor's building, and Ansel thought back to their very first visit. Everything still looked as pristine. They made their way up to the intercom. The large glass windows of the lobby gleamed in the sunlight, the way they had on the first visit. Trevor buzzed them up. They took the elevator again and exited the fourth floor. When they entered the apartment, however, they were surprised to find none other than Ally Beckman. She lay there, reclining on the sofa like a Modigliani. Her hair was tousled, spread about wildly, one leg scrunched, while the other hung off the sofa carelessly.

Trevor ushered them inside and introduced them to a guest who was seated on the sofa. Instead of feigning ignorance, Ansel pointed out that he and Luca were already well acquainted with Ally. Ansel turned to Ally and "what are you doing here?"

She sighed and gave a vague answer, "Trevor is an associate of mine." Trevor winked.

"Oh, how so?" Ansel pressed.

Ally seemed unsure of whether to answer. Trevor on the other hand, was forthcoming about their dealings. "Ally is my top dealer in the Pacific Northwest. She can move anything, weed, coke, X, without any issues."

Ansel could not believe the news but resolved not to let his emotions show. He turned to Luca but found only a look of utter astonishment on his friend's face. Ansel reverted his attention back to Ally, calmly pressing her for more information. He learned that Trevor played for the same lacrosse club as her brother, Ari. Initially Trevor had tried to recruit Ari, but Ari wasn't interested. Ally bragged that she made a much better candidate anyway, and Trevor agreed. Trevor explained that Ally routinely made pit stops in Oregon en route back to school, because his uncle had a facility there.

She provided the perfect cover—an innocent-looking, upper-middle class college girl. She looked racially ambiguous enough that police weren't going to hassle her. They could move however much pot or pills they wanted, without raising a hint of suspicion. Luca was absolutely stunned. Ally seemed intrigued by how the whole thing had played out, but Ansel remained placid. This whole endeavor was confirmation that Ally really was a lot like him and that he hadn't imagined the chemistry between them the night of her party. He was infinitely more curious about her, now that he knew she, too, broke the rules. Now that he knew that she, too, was living outside of the lines.

"Did you know that I worked for Trevor the night of your party?"

"Yes." Ally spoke in a tone that was straightforward but not still warm.

"Why don't we all sit down and have a smoke?" Trevor said, sensing some tension in the room. He disappeared into one of the back rooms and returned with a three-foot bong.

The gentlemen each settled on the loveseat, opposite of the sofa where Ally sat, while Ally made space for Trevor. She retrieved a stylish leather bag that was sitting on the coffee table to the side of her. She unzipped the bag and shuffled around inside for a minute, until she withdrew a densely packed sandwich bag. She opened it, took out a big crystal-covered green flower, and began to break it down in her fingertips. Ansel had visions of the night of her party. She was an expert at packing the bowl. She finished up and passed it. They all agreed she should take the first hit, so she did. She stood up, lit the stem, placed her lips on the mouth, and inhaled deeply. Billows of smoke rose inside the colorfully painted glass tube.

It had swirls of lavender and fuchsia, infused with splashes of magenta and bright red. Her graceful lips slid from the gargantuan piece, and she coolly exhaled a wondrous cumulous of smoke into the air. After his second turn, in what had grown to become somewhat comfortable silence, Ansel mustered the courage to ask Ally the burning question.

"What made you decide to get into this?"

"Probably for the same reason you did," she said, prancing over to him. She leaned down on the flank of the sofa nearest to him, and declared, "For the thrill of it."

She was a well-mannered beauty, with a dangerous side. She was as much in love with taking risks as him, although she'd painted herself as slightly more simplistic the night of her party. She'd known his secret. She hadn't said a word, but she knew he was dealing—maybe even that he wasn't in school somehow? Did she know that? She couldn't have, he thought, but again, he had once thought the same thing of Regina. Luca laid a hand on Ansel's shoulder, and tapped him out of his internal overanalytical spiral. Ansel gave his friend a look of sincere gratitude that was instantly understood. They went along casually talking with Ally and Trevor for another minute or two.

"So, Trevor says you're quitting?"

"Yup," Ansel said, trying to hide that he was surprised how much of Trevor's confidence she had. He had been working with Trevor for a year and a half, and still didn't speak to him much. When they spoke, it was the usual little niceties followed by business. He received updates on selling trends, gang violence, and territory disputes nearby. But they had never had a conversation that he deemed personal. Despite this, Ansel became more than a peddler. He had become part of an operation. His first month alone he'd moved more MDMA than the three other distributors on the East Coast combined.

Holly had often remarked that if he applied the same level of commitment to school, he'd graduate magna cum laude. And now there she was, Ally Beckman, goddess. She was in the same game as him, all the time without anyone knowing it. They continued to smoke and talk.

"I haven't been going to school much and my family knows," Ansel revealed. He didn't get much sympathy, but he hadn't really expected any either. He was more so stating it as a fact the only news he really had to share.

"That's wild. I'm going to have a half-sister soon," he said, shifting topics rather abruptly. "My dad's having another kid."

Ansel smiled and congratulated Trevor. Ally didn't say anything. Her being there was her revelation in and of itself. Meanwhile, Luca sat stiff as a mannequin. When the topic shifted again, Ansel ceased his moment.

"So, Trevor, I'm here because I want to get out of the business," he barely managed to say it without stuttering. Sweat poured down his forehead To Ansel's relief, Trevor understood why he wanted to get out of the business.

He assured Ansel there wouldn't be any issues. They had already wrapped up their last deal. "I'll make a call to Vince to let him know, and we'll get a replacement going for you."

Ansel suggested a former classmate, a kid he'd met in econ while he was still going to Walden. The kid had asked him about getting into "sales" as he called it. He was a freshman at Walden on a scholarship and told Ansel how much he needed the extra cash. For his part, Ansel hadn't made any promises. He told the kid that he would have to get permission to give his connection's (Trevor's) number out, and the choice was out of his hands. In that moment, sitting in Trevor's living room, Ansel was granted permission. He sent a text to his old classmate, and with that, he was out of the business.

Luca rose a bit hastily. "I have to get going, man," he said to Ansel.

"Sure," Ansel said, clumsily rising to leave with his friend. "All right, guys, it was nice seeing you." Luca walked even faster down the hall than he had out of the door.

"Luca, what's up, man? Why are you speeding off?"

Luca said nothing and continued walking until they were at the staircase. No elevator, this time, he was too much in a hurry. Panic was building in his footsteps. Ansel's legs began to throb as he tried to keep up. They were stoned, and he was practically chasing his friend down three flights of stairs. When they came to the lobby, Ansel finally shouted, "What the hell?"

"Sorry," Luca said, panting. "I had to get out. I'm sorry." They walked on leisurely toward the sidewalk. They crossed the street and entered Luca's car. He did not start it, but he put the key in the ignition. He stopped and turned to Ansel. "Since I knew one of your secrets, and I kept it to myself, I'm trusting you with what I'm about to say." Ansel nodded at Luca to signal he understood. Luca fidgeted and exhaled. He held it for a minute, and right when it seemed as though might turn blue and faint, he blurted out, "The night of the Beckman party, I had sex with Ari, and Ally walked in on us," he said.

"Oh my God," Ansel said, laughing. "Sorry for laughing. That's awful, but oh my god."

"We weren't having sex when she walked in. We were cuddling. But we were naked."

"Wow. That's a hot image."

"Shut up."

"So, wait, that whole time Ally knew I was selling dope, and that you had sex with her brother? I guess that explains why she was so comfortable telling us all about her involvement with Trevor and his uncle."

"She has nothing to lose." Luca laughed.

"I don't think she would say anything anyhow."

"Why are we both so attracted to danger?"

"Because we're from a shit town."

Luca finally started the car and they backed out of the space. They were driving at a much slower pace than usual for Luca. They talked on the way. Ansel learned Luca actually had a crush on Ari for a while. Luca and Ari had hooked up during a few of Ari's visits home from Washington. They kept in touch, friendly stuff. Ari came back this last time and they started something. It was casual. They were friends first. They sent each other text messages and still hung out in groups. It was still new, and neither of them had told anyone yet. Ally had walked in on them, holding each other, stark naked underneath gossamer bed sheets. She shrugged and walked away. Ari and Luca had been too drunk to care. But an hour or so later, the booze began to wear off and embarrassment set in. That's when Luca had found them, and he and Ansel left.

"You know the craziest part?" Luca said, staring off wistfully as he drove.

"What?" Ansel bubbled with curiosity.

"He said we had nothing to worry about because Ally already knows he's gay."

"Wow," was all Ansel managed to say. He had always taken Aris Beckman for a total ladies' man. He was surprised and intrigued to find out Ari wasn't even attracted to women at all.

"Yeah."

"Speaking of, not that one encounter has to change anything, but do you feel any different about your sexuality now? I mean, would you say you're..."

"I've been thinking a lot about that, even before hooking up with Ari. I'm like you. I think," sensing the direction in which is friend's question was headed, "bisexual."

"Awesome." They began to reach their sleepy little hometown. "What do you want to do when we get back?"

"Let's go to a bar. I could use a drink."

Chapter Ten

Two days had passed since the now infamous dinner, and the skin of Regina's cheek still stung. That night after Ansel had left the house and Elise was tucked away upstairs, Regina rose from the table without a word and headed for the kitchen. Once inside, she promptly retrieved a bag of split peas from the freezer. *Why is it always split peas?* How trite, how nineties TV drama of her to have to put a bag of split peas on her cheek, where her sister had slapped the hell out of her. Elise, pure as driven snow, had used violence as a means to get her point across.

Elise of Calcutta, Elise who never hurt a fly, had finally hit her breaking point. That was what had shocked Regina more than anything else. It was not being slapped itself; it was the fact that Elise had followed through. It was the fact that had Elise actually struck her. Regina realized instantly that her ego had taken a blow, right along with the side of her face. She had eventually journeyed away from the kitchen, upstairs, and into her room that night. After a minute or two, her mother got up and walked after her.

She approached Regina's room. Mrs. Wallis knocked twice, softly sounded out, "It's your mother," and entered the room before Regina could answer.

Regina had pulled the window open slightly. A cool breeze swept in through the room between the parted linen curtains. The incoming light gave the crimson walls an eerie glow. She sat on the edge of her childhood bed. Her mother sat down beside her. Mrs. Wallis placed a hand on Regina's shoulder.

"Is what your sister accused you of true?"

Out of excuses and unsure of what else to do, Regina looked up at her mother and answered plainly, "What do you think?"

Mrs. Wallis sighed deeply. "Well, that's unfortunate. You two used to be so close," she said. "I had hoped you would always remain so."

"Well, you can't always get what you want," Regina said. "Besides it was just sex; it didn't mean anything." She stood up and paced around.

"Darling, it may not have meant anything to you, but it did to your sister."

"But it shouldn't have," Regina exclaimed, throwing her hands up into the air out of frustration. It felt trivial to her to argue over sex and even more so because the person she'd slept with wasn't even in a committed relationship, or any sort of relationship at all for that matter, with her sister.

Mrs. Wallis walked over to her daughter. "But it did," she emphasized. "Can't you see why she might be upset, dear?"

Regina shifted her gaze away from her mother and off toward the bedroom window. "Of course," she said, "and you can stop talking to me in that tone. I'm not twelve." She had had enough with how condescending her mother was being. They both knew the perma-Zen attitude she had going on was bullshit. Still, she had a point. Regina hated to admit it, but their mother was right.

★

Downtown, Ansel was immersed introspection. He was seated at a table on the patio of a place called Bar Seven with Luca directly across from him. It was the coolest bar in Hunter, which wasn't saying much, since there were only a few bars in town anyway. Ansel and Luca were both drinking rum. Luca swirled his glass and took a few long sips in between telling Ansel all about Ari. It was in these intimate details that they bonded, for the first time in a long time. As Luca's story wound down Ansel's mind drifted.

He deduced that after ruminating on everything, Elise would have gone outside to get some air. Regina likely found some reason to leave the table after he did and would've been held up in her room, waiting for the inevitable talk from their mother about the attempt to blackmail him. He could see Elise, the peacemaker, traversing the stairs to his room in the hopes of chatting with him. Bracing herself at the door and knocking once, twice, maybe three times, before she turned the knob only to discover he was gone.

Ansel had had fun in Philly. He had made new friends and met a lot of people (mostly customers), but his social life was never quite like it was in Hunter. He had Holly, but that was it. Holly was usually preoccupied with school, her internship, and the occasional guy. It was when Sebastian came to visit that Ansel had realized that apart of him undeniably missed home. Home was where his friends were. These were the friends who knew everything about him, the friends who felt more like family than his actual family at times. Yet the reality was that home was still where his unhappiness lived, where his deceit and his failures made their nest. That reality had long coerced him out of staying.

However, Ansel realized, sitting at a table outside of Bar Seven, he had nothing to be scared of anymore. The truth was he could be sad, dishonest, and make mistakes far from home. He'd slept with Sebastian in Philly after all. It didn't matter where you were. Regretful moments could be born anywhere. Beautiful moments could arise anywhere. Yet he had spent his whole life running away every time something wasn't what he wanted it to be.

He knew that if he kept that up, he would never stop running. He broke from this revelry at the sound of his phone ringing. He saw the caller was Sebastian and sent the call to voicemail. Sebastian had been trying to contact him for the last two days, and he had ignored every call. He knew he had to answer eventually, but he wasn't ready to talk to Sebastian yet. Luca asked Ansel if there was anyone special in his life. Ansel's phone vibrated once more, as he started to reply.

He did not check to see who it was this time. He swirled his drink. "There might be, but it's complicated." They shared stories well into the night. At Ansel's request, Luca dropped him off at Isabelle's shortly before midnight. He figured it would be best to flat between the two of them, rather than impose on anyone for too long. Though Luca insisted that Ansel could continue staying with him without issue, Ansel would not take no for an answer. When he arrived, Isabelle buzzed him up. Ansel went to the staircase and fumbled halfway to the fifth floor, where Isabelle lived, before needing to stop.

He rested on the stairs and his phone vibrated again. The vibration made a louder, harder buzzing than usual from inside his pocket, since it was pushed up against the stairs beneath him. He took it out and peeked at the screen. It was a text from Sebastian. The message read:

> *Please call me. We need to talk about this some more.*

Ansel ignored it and his phone went off again. The next text simply read:

> *I'm pretty sure I'm in love with you.*

And with that, in his inebriated state, Ansel began to weep. He did not make much noise, but the crying took all his breath, and all his strength away. He cried for the loss of his grandfather. He cried for the loss of respect between his sisters and at the pathetic relationship he had with his mother. He had been running from the decay of his life at home for so long, hoping maybe if he separated himself from it, it would fade.

All he needed was time and space, he had thought. Yet, there they were after two whole years of time and space between them, and they still couldn't stand to be all together under one roof. Ansel thought about the fact that Sebastian may well be in love with him, and he began sobbing because all he knew of love was what he had learned from his family. And what he had learned was that love came with inevitable hurt and betrayal. *What a mess*, he thought, gripping his sides.

He melted into the wall beside him, into the stairs beneath him, until silence washed back in like the tide. Once he had pulled himself together and wiped the tears from his eyes, he went inside Isabelle's apartment. He rinsed his face in the bathroom sink to rid it of any evidence that he'd been upset. That night, Ansel slept sounder than he could ever recall.

Chapter Eleven

He awoke on the morning of June 1 at eleven-thirty to five missed calls and seven text messages from Sebastian. Ansel decided not to read the messages. Instead, he prepared for his official meeting with Elise. He had decided he was going to stay for at least a few more weeks, maybe until school started in Philly. His phone buzzed, Sebastian again; he continued to ignore the alerts. But he realized something, after glancing at his phone and seeing the date.

It was June 1: that meant he had only been in Hunter for six days. Six days and his biggest secret had turned out to be nothing at all. He'd learned his sisters hated each other and one of his best friends had betrayed him, then professed his love—it was all so much and all in under a week. Even at eleven thirty, he was still up before Isabelle. He went into the guest bathroom and took a shower. When he finished getting ready, he left quietly. He decided he would text her after the meeting with his sister was over.

He strolled down to Avery Boulevard and caught the bus to the furthest point possible. Before he got off, he called a taxi, and it arrived minutes after he departed with the bus. He took the cab the rest of the way. They arrived at the old colonial, and he paid the driver. With the morning light shining upon it, the house was more beautiful than Ansel had ever remembered. Consciously, he had always known it was a beautiful house, but he hadn't thought about it in a long time. He'd lived in it, attended parties held in it by his parents, but he had never really felt he belonged in it.

He'd never felt like he belonged in Hunter. He had gone to Philly to separate himself from more than just his dysfunctional family. He had gone to separate himself from their whole world. He had grown up around money, but he hadn't had money. It was always clear to him that he had to earn whatever he wanted.

His mom would pay for college, but he would have to find a job and an apartment on his own. He hadn't minded that in the slightest; he'd yearned for that sort of independence his whole life. Funny, how you can want something for so long, and still not know what to do once you have it. He had gained physical independence from his family and from the town once he'd moved away, yet still he needed them. He was tied to the town whether he liked it or not. He had been tied to the town, but not anymore. It had all started with the old colonial, and now it was all ending with it.

Chapter Twelve

When Mrs. Wallis had first married Ansel's father, they were young and hopeful. Her dance career was flourishing, and Mr. Wallis had happily begun his teaching career at a small private school across town. They drank wine at fetching restaurants and danced along the shoreline at night. A year into the marriage they had Elise, closely followed by Regina two years later. Both of their girls exhibited genius tendencies at early ages. Mrs. Wallis and her late husband spent hours teaching their children everything they could, from spelling to arithmetic, to the laws of modern physics. The girls were reading by the time they were each a year old.

Elise was dancing and Regina sculpting figurines from clay by two and four years old respectively. They had a wonderful family, and they were joyous. They still drank wine and danced together along the shore, but they had to hire a sitter. Four years after Regina, they had Ansel. Mrs. Wallis had begun traveling with her dance troupe more and felt extremely guilty about leaving home so much.

She missed her children, she missed her husband, and yet she resented those feelings. It felt like Atlas's burden, weighing down her soul. She could feel it rising inside her like a tropical storm every time anyone asked her how things were going. It came and went, but each time it felt stronger and stronger, like it had picked up more wind, more rain than the last time. Soon enough she envisioned herself growing into a hurricane. Her mother had been a hurricane after all. While Mrs. Wallis was battling with inner turmoil, Mr. Wallis was thriving.

They hired a nanny and still drunk wine on occasion, but they hardly ever danced together anymore. They were both constantly working instead. He was engrossed in grading papers, and she consumed by rehearsals. This was, of course, when they weren't both attending one of Elise's recitals, or Regina's openings. As the girls' careers grew on, so did their demand for attention. With Mr. Wallis being the breadwinner, caring for the children fell primarily to Mrs. Wallis, and her resentment only swelled because of it. As Thanksgiving of ninety-two rolled around, Mr. Wallis thought it would be a good idea for the family to go on a vacation.

He rented a cabin at Lake Tahoe, and the family made the two-hour trip there with plans to stay for a few weeks. The first week was magical, the second week things had become a bit trying, and on the fourth day of the third week the kids begged to go ice-skating. Mrs. Wallis at first refused due to malaise. However, when she saw how full of wonder the children were, she couldn't deny them. Ansel was six years old at the time, so Mr. and Mrs. Wallis both gripped each of his hands tightly as they led their kids across the frozen lake. Regina and Elise laughed as they clutched each other for balance.

Ansel skated gleefully between his parents, ice chips fluttering behind him, until Mr. Wallis's phone rang. As he stepped away to answer it, young Ansel darted off on his own and lost balance. Of course, Mrs. Wallis's first instinct was to run after her son. Forgetting momentarily that she was on skates, she tripped and heard a loud cracking as she landed. A shrill pang ran out throughout her left ankle. As she cried out in pain, Mr. Wallis dropped his phone and skated after her.

The girls skated toward their mother as well, while a confused and scared Ansel looked on. She had initially thought she merely twisted her ankle, but as the hissing pain had evolved into an excruciating agony, Mrs. Wallis knew something was wrong. She gasped for air, feeling the coolness of the frost and snow around her. Mr. Wallis tried to lift her up, but the slightest pressure on her left foot made her scream and howl. Eventually he was able to get her upright. He brought her inside the cabin for hot cocoa and wrapped her up in blankets.

After that, all Mrs. Wallis could remember was a doctor telling her that she had fractured her ankle and her foot in several places. It would require surgery, but the doctor was certain that her foot would heal all right. Yet sadly, given the severity of the injury, there was no guarantee it would ever be safe for her to dance professionally again. It would take six to eight weeks of recovery time post-surgery, but Mrs. Wallis knew her career was over. Once limbs have broken, they never quite heal the same way.

The curtain closed with her face down on the ice. In the days immediately following the accident, Mrs. Wallis existed in a permanent state of lamentation. Her husband tried desperately to reassure her that everything would be all right, but it only angered her. one night at dinner, he uttered the phrase "look at the bright side." Before he finished, she threw him a deathly glare, parted her lips to utter five simple words into the cold, crisp air:

"Are you fucking kidding me?"

Her husband paused; Elise paused, mouth agape; Regina delighted at hearing a swear word; and Ansel was on the verge of tears. Mrs. Wallis apologized to her children. She never intended to, but she grew distant from everything around her more and more after that. She was there, but not fully engaged. This emotionally vacant state lasted for many years.

She did not know at the time that Ansel blamed himself for her injury, having been the cause of the accident. It was one of the reasons he had attempted suicide. He was officially diagnosed with depression by age thirteen. No one in the family discussed it with him. Instead, Mrs. Wallis promptly enrolled her son in therapy. Unfortunately, seeing a therapist only made Ansel feel like more of a problem to the rest of the family. Mrs. Wallis learned this by reading Ansel's journals. Through the journals, she also discovered that he daydreamed about dying. These fantasies focused not on the physical act of death itself, so much as the idea of permanent nonexistence. When he wasn't writing about his longing for death, he was consumed by loneliness. Fortunately, this was at the same time that Sebastian transferred to his school. As Mrs. Wallis read on week after week, she grew relieved ro see things change. Ansel finally had a real friend, someone he turned to.

However, instead of seeking out therapy or a friend, Mrs. Wallis immersed herself in a myriad of activities to help her cope: book clubs, wine, online language classes.

She had come a long way from the grief-stricken woman she'd been in the wake of the accident. There was still melancholy in her eyes, but she had hardened.

She headed into the living room to face her family. There they were. Elise, her eldest, was making herself a drink at the bar. Elise gave off the impression of being happy and well-adjusted, aside from hating Regina.

Her youngest, Ansel, leaned against the interior doors that led to the kitchen. He stared out at nothing. She wondered what her son was thinking. What he was feeling. He never spoke to her about those kinds of things. He had a whole life in Philadelphia she was completely unaware of, except that he was willing to put on a charade in order to protect it.

Mrs. Wallis peered off out to the garden and saw Regina standing there, right in front of the doorway to the living room. Regina smoked a cigarette. *How I wish she would give up that nasty habit.* The universe granted her wish, albeit momentarily, when Regina put out her cigarette and came inside. They gathered around, and Mrs. Wallis broke the silence. "Let's get on with it, shall we?"

Their attorney stood up and walked over to the fireplace. "I hear we have a transference of property."

Ansel reached into a black messenger bag resting on the floor beside him. "That's correct." He pulled out the documents transferring his share of the house over to Elise. The attorney took the paperwork, read it over, and gave a pleased look. Elise looked up, sipped her vodka tonic, and moved a few stray hairs out of her line of vision. The attorney walked over to her and placed the papers down on the bar. She took hold of them and stared off for a minute.

"I guess this means we'll be keeping this house," Mrs. Wallis said.

"No," Elise proclaimed sharply. "I've changed my mind. I don't want Ansel's shares. I'd prefer to sell." None of the glass in the room shattered; no one fainted; no one hardly even said a word after Elise declared that she, too, wanted to sell the house. They all stood there in silent agreement and watched the attorney pulled a second set of paperwork out of his briefcase. He had apparently drafted the documents at Elise's request the evening before. She had been thinking of going this route since their last family dinner together. Signing the documents to agree to sell the old colonial took all of seven minutes.

After the attorney had gone, the Wallises all stood quietly in the living room for a moment. Unexpectedly, and rather uncharacteristically, Mrs. Wallis began to cry. The tears came in rivulets, accompanied by a deep, mournful sobbing. Her family stood there frozen in their tracks, staring at her. She sat herself down on the ivory sofa. Finally, after a minute or two of carrying on, Regina walked over, sat beside her mother, and held her.

Ansel watched as Mrs. Wallis leaned her head gracefully on his sister's shoulder and continued weeping. He drifted away into another memory he had thought was long forgotten. He was thirteen and it was autumn. It had been raining heavily all day. He had received a ride home from Sebastian's mom, because his own mother hadn't picked up her phone. He walked into the house and called out to see if anyone was home. There was no reply.

By that time, Elise and Regina had already moved to New York City. He and his mother were the only residents of the house. Ansel strolled upstairs, through the hallway, and made out classical music emanating from his mom's bedroom. As he made his way further down the hall, he observed a loud sobbing as well. He trotted carefully, mindful of the sound each footstep made, until he came to their bedroom door. He turned the knob gently to find his mother in bed. She was fully clothed, sitting on the neatly folded duvet, with mascara running down both sides of her face.

She'd stopped crying as soon as she had detected the doorknob turning. She froze at first. She took a moment, cleared her throat, and asked him how school was. He told her it was fine. She offered no explanation for her tears, told him to go read, and asked if he could shut the door behind him. He did as she requested, and never asked her why she had been crying. The question nagged him for weeks, but he could not figure out a way to bring it up to her.

He'd eventually decided to let it go, and they never spoke of the incident again. He was thrust back into the present with the sound of Regina's voice.

"What's the matter?" Regina asked their mother calmly.

"This house was the last thing keeping this family together."

"But you wanted to sell from the beginning," Ansel said.

"Yes," Mrs. Wallis answered, in between lessening sobs, "and I still do. I'm glad we've all agreed to put this place on the market. It just hurts. It hurts to know that my children can't stand each other. It hurts to know they don't come to me for help or talk to any of us about how they feel. It hurts to know that we've come to a point where Elise doesn't even want to fight to keep this place anymore. After everything that's happened since William's death, I've realized that much like my marriage, it couldn't be fixed." It had finally happened; after years of being wound up so tight, their mother had unraveled. Regina held her mother until the tears subsided. "I know what you're going to say," Mrs. Wallis eventually said.

"What's that, Mother?"

"Finally, something other than a goddamn smile!"

Regina smiled wide and her mother let out a little laugh.

"I thought I was making the right choices," Mrs. Wallis said. "I didn't want to set a poor example for you girls, but I also didn't want to be another statistic 'single black mother in America,'" she scoffed. "So, I put up with your father's cheating, I bore the loss of my career, and I smiled through it all. Ansel, I knew you wanted attention. I meant to give it to you, I tried, but it was so hard raising two prodigies. Raising children is a full-time job alone. Raising children with bustling careers was twice the workload. God, I wanted to be a stronger person, but I couldn't."

"We know, Mother, and we know you feel responsible, but this isn't all your fault. This is the way it is."

Ansel rose, walked over to Elise, and embraced her. She whispered that she loved him, and he reciprocated the sentiment. Regina was next but didn't say anything. She wrapped her arms around him. After a few moments, it was his mother's turn. Mrs. Wallis held on to him tighter than he remembered in a long time. For a moment, he was six years old again and had scraped his knee playing in the driveway.

He could feel the dirt caked around his knee. The salty ground stung in his open wound. He saw his mother running toward him, heard the nervousness in her voice. She embraced him. He could feel her warmth and worry all at the same time, her comfort and sadness. Emotions swept over him like an incoming tide. He whispered an apology into his mother's ear, tears streaming down his face.

"Oh, my darling, I'm the one who's sorry." She dabbed at her eyes. "I never meant to take it out on you."

Ansel patted his mother's shoulder, dried his eyes, and walked out. Silence fell upon the room again, and the last light of day streamed in through the doors that led to the garden.

Chapter Thirteen

Ansel walked four blocks, under oak trees shimmying in the summer breeze. He came to the cul-de-sac at the end of the road, where a well-kept Tudor-style house stood in the middle of two other houses. He went around the back of the Tudor, came across a tennis ball, picked it up, and tossed it at the outer left window on the second story. After one or two tosses, he saw hands lift the window from the pane, and Sebastian peered out. He did not say a word. He didn't even shut the window. Within a moment or two, he had come down the stairs and out of a set of large French glass doors into the backyard.

"You're supposed to throw pebbles."

"Says who? Plus, I didn't want to risk breaking your window."

"So you went with a tennis ball instead?"

"Don't you want to know why I am here?"

"Why are you here? You wouldn't return my calls or texts and I..."

Before Sebastian could finish, Ansel walked over to him and gave him an intense kiss on the lips. "You saved me. Thank you."

"What do you mean?"

"Now that everything is out in the open, my family and I were able to come to an agreement to sell the house." He was elated and trembling with excitement as he relayed the information. When he finished, he noticed Sebastian was quiet and still. Ansel wanted to stretch forward and caress his cheek. He wanted to take hold of Sebastian's hands, stroke his hair, and do anything to comfort him. Yet Ansel was afraid to move, afraid he'd take a step too soon.

"So that's it, huh?"

"Were you expecting something else?"

"No, yes. Look, I know I shouldn't have told your mom about school, but..." Sebastian hesitated for a moment. He was either searching for the right words or safe words to supplant them. "I care about you a lot." The phrase tasted lackluster as it rolled off his tongue.

"I know," Ansel said, not paying any recognition to Sebastian's earlier hesitation.

"So what, are you going to stay and look for an apartment?"

"I'm not certain yet. I wish I was, but I'm not. I'm sorry."

Sebastian gave an understanding nod, kissed Ansel once more, and whispered, "You're an asshole," in his ear.

"I know."

They stood there face-to-face as a tear slid down Sebastian's cheek. Ansel continued to apologize. He didn't know what else to say. It was the first real instance in which he felt his heart breaking at the exact same time as someone else's. It was also the first time he truly understood why it was called heartbreak. It felt like his heart valves were closing in tight, his ribs would soon shatter, and the whole damn thing could come bursting out of his chest at any minute. But he knew it was a sacrifice that had to be made; it was the right thing to do.

Sebastian ran a hand across Ansel's forehead, through his hair, and down over his face. They kissed again and Sebastian took Ansel by the hand. Ansel followed as Sebastian led him into the house. The lights were dim, no one had been home except Sebastian, and so they stayed in the living room. They sat on the sofa at first but wound up on the floor, soft hazel carpet underneath them as they kissed and embraced. Their fingers traced each other's sides, up and down each other's spines.

They bit at each other's lips. The air and their movements tinged with a sweaty teenaged nervousness. Sebastian broke away, woke the computer in the corner, and hit the random play button. As it so happened, that became the first time that either of them had ever made love to the Beatles. Skin on skin. Hands roaming, tender kisses everywhere, and a bite and a howl in between. When they were finished, they lay in each other's arms.

Words were not needed, nor wanted. Instead, they let the magnetism that had always existed between them sweep over them. Two hours later, Ansel rose to leave. He and Sebastian handed each other the articles of clothing they had discarded. They embraced once more, heads resting on each other's shoulders, like they had the rest of their lives to be there. Of course, they knew that moment could not last forever, so it went the way of all good things, and Ansel left. He strolled off away from Sebastian's and endeavored on the long walk back to where he would catch the bus downtown.

He called Luca when he arrived on Avery Boulevard. Luca showed up in short order. They rode with the music turned down low, and Ansel shared everything that had happened.

"I'm proud of you," Luca said at the end of it.

"Thanks," Ansel said.

Luca fiddled with the car stereo, and "Martha My Dear" flooded in through the speakers. It was a cruel coincidence. Night had fallen and the sky had become an abyss, save for the few twinkling stars that you could still make out in the glow of the city lights.

Chapter Fourteen

Ansel awoke at Isabelle's apartment the next day, around two in the afternoon, to a dull ache in the pit of his stomach. He ignored it, called Luca, and together with Isabelle, they went to a gay bar called Pilot, which was right outside of town. Ansel and Luca joked about how Isabelle was their token straight friend, until Isabelle reminded them that she identified as sexually fluid. They all had a drink. One turned into two; two turned into three. Before Ansel knew it, the sky was swaying and the ground beneath his feet felt like liquid.

They sat in the back of the room, in the midst of a decent crowd. Though he was drunk, Ansel was relatively all right, until he realized that the bar was playing a song by the Beatles. Tears flowed from his eyes. He wasn't sobbing loud and heavy, but his tears streamed steadily. He looked around and noticed all the couples gazing into each other's eyes lovingly. With his index finger tucked between his teeth and his fist covering his mouth, Ansel trembled a bit. He grimaced, trying to make it stop.

Luca put an arm around one of Ansel's shoulders. Isabelle put hers around the other, and they sat there until Ansel composed himself. They all took a shot of tequila.

Ansel drank some water and dried his eyes. The group split the bill and staggered onto the street.

"Home, gentlemen?" Isabelle asked.

"Fuck no," Luca laughed.

Ansel and Isabelle erupted into laughter as well. They wandered for a few blocks, until Ansel suggested they head to the nearby public library. Luca protested that the library was closed, but Isabelle reminded him that they were going up onto the roof. The night was warm. They made it to the library without incident, which was miraculous in the state they were in.

The three walked around back, and each took turns hopping on top of the closed dumpster in order to get to the ladder that led to the rooftop. Although inebriated, they could have repeated these steps a thousand times in the dark, as they had done it at least that many times growing up. It was their "spot." The building itself was gargantuan in width, and two stories high. Since most of Hunter had been flat when they were growing up, with the exception of downtown, the library presented a good vantage point for a spectacular view of the city. But the high-rise apartment buildings that had proliferated in the last two years blocked off that view.

Still, the three friends were still together underneath the moonlit sky, and that was good enough for them. They sat cross-legged on the rooftop.

"My mom's getting remarried," Isabelle said.

"What? To whom?" Ansel asked.

"Some insurance adjuster she met in Italy. She got into a minor accident in a rental car there last fall. It was love at first claims report. They've been together since," Isabelle said.

"What's he like?" Luca asked.

"I don't know," Isabelle revealed. "Truth be told, I haven't met him yet. In fact, I only learned of his existence via email. Anyway, my mother is leaving me the apartment. The next two months are paid for, but after that I'm on our own."

"What the hell?" Ansel said. "What are you going to do?"

"I'll be all right," Isabelle said. "I have some money saved, and I'll be entering a nursing program soon."

"Maybe we can go apartment hunting together," Ansel added, prompting Luca to ask whether he would be returning to Philadelphia. Ansel sighed loudly. "I don't know," he said, his voice dripping with apathy. "I wanted to this whole time, but now that I'm not in school anymore, I have no obligation to keep up the charade."

"Well, you and Isabelle can always stay with me if you need to. You guys are family."

Luca half-slurred his words, "And I'm not just saying that because I'm drunk."

Isabelle laughed heartily at Luca's presentation. "I know, and thanks man." She placed an arm around Ansel's shoulder. "At least you'll have some money from the sale of the house."

"Yeah, but what happens when that runs out?"

"God, I hate thinking about the future," Luca interjected.

Having sensed there was more to that statement, Ansel prodded Luca to elaborate. Luca tried to play it off as a harmless comment, but Ansel knew better. He pressed Luca again to open up. "Spill it."

"Spill what?" Luca asked.

"You know we won't stop harassing you until you tell us," Isabelle said. The wind picked up and swept across the open rooftop.

Luca paused for a long while and stared into the open air. "Okay, I also received shitty news this week," he said. "It's Ari. Apparently, there's a new person on the cleaning staff at his house. They found half a kilo of cocaine in his room and snitched to his parents. I guess they didn't want to get blamed for it, who knows? Anyway, Ari's parents are sending him to rehab in a week."

"I'm sorry, Luca," Ansel said, knowing how close the two had grown.

"I'm grateful that he's going to see help and all, but I guess I really like him, Luca said.

"Wait, what, Ari is gay?" Isabelle said.

Ansel had been so self-absorbed he hadn't realized Luca had confided only in him about Ari. He knew the impact keeping a secret like that could have on one's psyche. He gave Ari a glance that said, you'd better tell her, and with that Luca began to explain.

"Honestly, I only ever thought of him as a friend, until the night after his welcome home party. I don't even remember what led to it, but we ended up talking outside in the Beckmans' massive backyard and we kissed. He kissed me, I should say. Things developed slowly from there. It was strictly casual at first, but we wound up spending real quality time together."

"And now you like him. Makes sense," Isabelle said. She had to wipe a few loose strands of hair from her face due to the drafty weather.

"Well, his parents are giving him a week, right?" Ansel said.

"Yeah, they won't be back from Turks and Caicos until then. They want to personally escort him to the airport," Luca said.

"You know what I say, I say make the most of the time you guys have together," Ansel said, raising his hand wildly in the air. Luca nodded in acknowledgment that Ansel was right. The three friends stretched out and lay flat on the roof. They stared at the stars, until starlight became morning light. They crept down the ladder and back onto the street a little after sunrise and continued on to Isabelle's apartment.

Luca was parked out front. Ansel and Isabelle both hugged Luca goodbye and headed off toward the lobby of her mother's apartment building. As she put her key in the lock of the glass lobby door, she turned to Ansel. "Why weren't you shocked at the news that Ari Beckman was gay?"

Ansel replied with a question of his own, "why weren't you surprised to learn Luca had feelings for a guy?"

Isabelle chuckled. "Touché." She opened the lobby door.

As they entered the ground floor of the building, Luca heading off to his car, fading into the distance.

Ansel later found out that Luca took his advice and went to the Beckman house to see Ari. They spent the night cuddling in bed together, while Ansel lay spread out on a sofa in Holly's mother's living room. He had just stepped into Luca's apartment, after the long night atop the roof of the library, when Holly called him. It was time for her to head back to Philadelphia to prepare for fall semester. He slept until 9:30 a.m., went over to her house to say goodbye. As things usually went with the two, they wound up talking about everything that had recently happened to them. Since she had been back from Walden, Holly had taken up exotic dancing a few nights a week at a lounge in Santa Monica.

In her own words, she had to "continue the love affair that ignited and flourished in Philly." As she described it, she was entertaining the crowd in a red lacy number, and right as she flung her sheer stockings off stage, the unexpected happened. "Derrick, the dental hygienist from my mother's office, came in," she said.

"Shit, so she's going to find out?"

"The hell she will. I gave him a lap dance as part of my act."

"You didn't."

"I certainly did! What's he going to say to my mother now? 'Your daughter is stripping for a living,'" she scoffed. "'She was grinding in my lap last night.'"

"Good point," Ansel said.

Holly asked what he was planning to do with his life, and Ansel confessed that he didn't know. She stared at him, soaking in the nervousness, the anguish he felt. He didn't know where he was headed, or what he was going to be. Holly blinked. "In a perfect world, what would you like to happen?" she asked.

"In a perfect world? I'd have my friends and Sebastian and Philly. I'd have it all."

"Figure out a way to make that happen."

He wanted to scream that it wasn't possible, but he knew what she would say. *Nothing is impossible.* He buried his chin in his hands. "If I go back to Philly, I have to give up everyone here. If I stay behind, I have to give up Philly," he said.

"Not true. Your friends will still be here for you. I'll still be here for you," she said.

Damn it, she's right, he brooded. He was dumbfounded. She summed everything up so perfectly, and it was all there, right before his eyes all along. He had been looking at things all wrong. He had been gone two and a half years. Each time he visited it was like nothing changed with his friends in Hunter. Even with major developments happening in their lives, they were still a constant source of love and support. He knew he wouldn't lose Holly because she was always true to her word. Yet, he had believed he would have to lose something. This wasn't the case with the people in his life. Lying there on Holly's mother's sofa, he realized the question wasn't, *what am I willing to lose?* The question was, *where do I go from here?* He sat up just as his phone vibrated. He checked it and rose from the sofa completely. He walked over to Holly and gave her a hug. "I've got to go. Call me when you land?"

"Of course," she said, "and tell Sebastian I said hi." She gave Ansel that omniscient look again.

"Sure thing," Ansel said, unabashed. It wasn't until several blocks later, when he arrived at the gargantuan bookstore on Fourth Street, that Ansel realized the implications Holly had made at their parting. He could not deny that he had been thinking about Sebastian. He had been without much rest since their last encounter. However, he was also quite determined not to make a decision he couldn't undo. That was why he had not gone off to see Sebastian. Instead, he went to meet Isabelle.

Isabelle had sent him a text message, stating she had some important news for him. He made his way through the ground floor. There was a security guard at the entrance, across from a big golden escalator that led to the other two floors of the store. Smooth jazz spouted from speakers hidden in each corner of the building. Ansel headed to the second floor and walked over to a row of windows that overlooked Avery Boulevard. He noticed Isabelle standing a few feet away and went over to her.

She was dressed impeccably per usual. She had on a teal top with fringe down the middle, which complemented her bronze skin. She also wore a satin sash around her waist that led to a black knee-length pencil skirt. She stood there patiently, with her pea coat in hand. "So, what's so important?" Ansel asked, approaching her.

"I have something to say, and you're not going to like it," Isabelle said. She was nothing if not honest. It was one of the many facets of her personality he so deeply admired.

"Well, skip to it," Ansel said, sitting down in a nearby reading chair.

"I'm the one who told Regina that you weren't going to college," she stuttered. "I wanted you to stay in Hunter. I needed you to stay."

"What the hell, Issy? That is not okay," Ansel said, raising his voice.

"You don't understand," she said, her voice straining. She tried to reach out to him, but he swiftly moved out of the way. She gulped for air and tried to keep her composure.

"You betrayed me. You went behind my back and did something that you knew I wouldn't want you to do. You've been lying to me by omission since I've been here," he said, fuming.

Isabelle caught her breath. "I'm sorry."

"No, I'm sorry," Ansel said. "I have to go." He stormed off. He had hardly made it back down to the ground floor of the building before receiving a text from Isabelle begging to let her explain. Ansel couldn't deal with it. He knew he had to hear her out eventually, but he was too upset to give her an answer. He walked and walked until he found himself in the last place he had expected to go, Sebastian's house. Ansel entered Sebastian's backyard through the side of the house, then sent Sebastian a text message asking him to come outside. Within minutes, Sebastian came out to the yard and sat on the grass cross-legged. Ansel laid his head in his friend's lap, and Sebastian ran his fingers through Ansel's hair. "I'm sorry for just showing up like this," Ansel started.

"Don't be," Sebastian said, instantaneously making Ansel feel safe. "What happened?" he asked. He continued stroking Ansel's hair, and though Ansel did feel safe and warm, he could sense the anxiety in Sebastian's voice. It was unnerving coming from someone who was always so calm and collected. Still, Ansel shared the whole story and Sebastian listened carefully. When it was over, he asked

Ansel whether Isabelle had shared her reasons for telling Regina his secret.

Ansel glanced up, staring into Sebastian's spellbinding eyes. "She said she needed me to stay in Hunter," he said softly. "But I didn't let her finish."

Sebastian tried to hold back his annoyance, but he couldn't help himself. "So, you wanted to know what her motive was, but you didn't let her explain herself?"

"Counterproductive, I know," Ansel said, barely sensing Sebastian's irritation. "But I just couldn't hang around to find out."

"You let your emotions cloud your judgment. You did the same thing with me when you found out that I let it slip to your mom that you weren't in school."

Ansel sat up. "That was wrong of you," he said, his forehead furrowing. His voice had grown sharp and serious.

"Just like it was wrong of you to lie to them in the first place?" Sebastian said. His voice, too, had grown serious, and his words shot out hot like lava and oozed over Ansel's skin.

Ansel took a breath and tried to reply with as much affection as he could muster. "You're not helping, sweetheart."

"Are you going to storm out of here?" Sebastian said. He was beyond a kind word and beyond sparing Ansel's feelings. All he had done, all anyone close to Ansel had ever done, was spare his feelings. Enough was enough.

"Don't do that," Ansel said. It was half plea, half warning.

"What, predict your next move?" Sebastian said, his tongue dripping with vitriol.

Ansel stood up. "You're being an ass," he said, crossing his arms. Sebastian, too, stood up, and Ansel deliberately moved away from him.

"And you're being a child. Go find out what Issy has to say. You've known her for years. You at least owe her that much."

"Let's get something straight. I don't owe anyone anything," Ansel said, looking Sebastian in the eyes. "It was my secret to tell, not yours, not hers, not Regina's—mine."

"Okay, I understand that. But you said yourself that you want to know why she told Regina, so why not go find out?"

"I'm not ready yet," Ansel acquiesced. He could never stay upset at Sebastian for long, especially not when they were face-to-face. It was so much harder for Ansel to resist him when he could hear Sebastian's voice and feel his presence. Sebastian didn't let him down easy, though, and accused him as gently as possible of running from a difficult situation yet again. Ansel wondered why Sebastian seemed so invested in repairing his and Isabelle's friendship. It hit him, that old familiar pang of fear that Sebastian wasn't being completely honest. He pressed Sebastian for the missing pieces of the puzzle.

Sebastian looked away. He had not expected Ansel to turn the tables. He had not expected Ansel to know he was harboring anything, but of course Ansel knew him better than anyone. They were transparent to each other, for better or worse.

"I'm not running now. I'm right here asking you what you know."

"It's not my secret to tell," Sebastian said, half-sarcastic, half-serious. He didn't care that it burned. He had vacillated from love to anger to love and back again.

Ansel acknowledged this. He couldn't pretend he didn't deserve it. He had treated Sebastian the same. "I think it's a little too late for discretion."

"Fine. Isabelle was hospitalized," Sebastian blurted out. "She was under a lot of pressure with school, her mom, her job, and it pushed her over the edge. She went to St. Joseph's on a seventy-two-hour hold. She had just been released a few days or so before you returned. She only told Regina, because she wanted you to stay. You went through the same thing. She knew you'd understand."

"This doesn't make any sense. Why didn't she just tell me?"

"It sounds like she tried to."

"Well now, I have to…"

"Go? I know; get out of here already," Sebastian said. He rolled his eyes, Ansel kissed his cheek, and they embraced. It felt natural yet odd at the same time. They hadn't concluded anything about the future of their relationship, or whether there even was a relationship beyond their years as friends, but Sebastian didn't care. He let himself melt into Ansel, and Ansel did the same. When Ansel had calmed, he quietly left.

★

One forty-five-minute taxi ride later, Ansel had arrived downtown. The trip has been a blur of lights: yellow, red, and that ever-elusive green. When he arrived at Avery

Boulevard, he took a deep breath and exited the cab. He walked around the corner to Rosewood Avenue. Once he was standing at Luca and Isabelle's apartment building, he sent Isabelle a text message. Five minutes later, she was downstairs standing right in front of him, expressing how sorry she was.

"I know," he said. His tongue felt thicker and heavier than it had before. He struggled, swallowed hard, and continued, "I'm sorry I didn't hear you out. Sebastian told me what happened."

"I figured that would happen sooner or later," she said, sighing and looking away.

Ansel hesitated. He could feel the proverbial knot in his stomach tense and twist as he searched for the right words. "I could've been here sooner," he said, "if I had known."

"It all happened so fast. Besides, I didn't expect you to drop everything and come home."

"You knew I wasn't going to school. There was nothing to drop," he said, letting out a nervous laugh. He hadn't necessarily intended to, but he had lightened the mood.

"Still," she said, fighting back a smile, "the timing didn't seem right, with your granddad and all. I assumed the worst Regina would do was tell your mom, and she'd make you stick around." Isabelle paused and looked up at the sky. The clouds swirled in the vast, mysterious blue. "I should've just told you," she said after a minute or two.

"You had your reasons," Ansel answered. In that moment, he saw all the years he had known Isabelle play out before his eyes. He saw their first year in high school. Sebastian had introduced them in the quad, and Ansel later realized that Isabelle was in his AP History class. She was the student who knew the answers to all the difficult questions, so naturally she was bored with the curriculum. Her grace, the way she spoke was cool and refined.

The way she stood, sat, and walked—all regal. She jarred him on their first in-class encounter with each other. The students had been split in two teams in preparation for a debate. She and Ansel were placed as captains of the opposing teams. After Isabelle's team won, she invited Ansel to eat lunch with her that afternoon. Luca joined them. He and Ansel hit it off right away.

Luca introduced him to Isabelle, who had gone to junior high with him. The rest was history. The rest was Issy kicking Patrick Rowe in the gonads for tripping Luca in the hall. It was the way she ran over to Ansel shrieking after Luca's party, when he was passed out in the Herrings' backyard. She was the first to call him after Ansel had attempted to take his own life. She made a mistake this once, but she had always been there for him—for them all. He couldn't say the same for himself. He was exactly the way Sebastian had described him. Ready to take flight at any moment, avoidant, and quick to judgment. He inhaled deeply and decided he was done being that way, starting right then and there. Isabelle draped her arm around Ansel's shoulder.

"Now, that we got all this mushy stuff out of the way, come on up," she said. "You're still staying with me."

"Aye-aye," Ansel said, laughing.

Chapter Fifteen

Once he was safely inside Isabelle's apartment, Sebastian came to mind. Ansel called and the phone rang a couple of times, before he caught Sebastian's voice on the other end. They said their hellos, and Sebastian stated he had something important to say.

"Uh-oh," Ansel joked. He walked toward the sliding door that led out to Isabelle's balcony and stepped outside. "What's up?" he said.

"I'm glad you came over today," Sebastian said, a bit sad. "I'm glad you feel like you can come to me in general, but I can't be there for you right now. I can't be anything for anyone right now."

"Okay," Ansel said. He discerned the seriousness in Sebastian's voice. He wanted to end the conversation there, to say he understood and let Sebastian go, but he couldn't. "What brought that on, if I may ask?"

"I suppose I ruminated on matters more," Sebastian remarked.

Ansel tried arguing. They'd been together only a couple of hours ago, but he wasn't surprised to learn that Sebastian hadn't stopped thinking about the state of their relationship after their hook-up over spring break. "What exactly does all of this mean to you?" He hated himself for asking immediately after he had done it. He yearned to know and yet he didn't.

Sebastian merely sighed. "I don't just want to be a hook-up. Our friendship, our presence in each other's lives is more important to me than that, more sacred."

Again, Ansel considered arguing that he hadn't done anything to make Sebastian feel this way, at least not deliberately, but he realized there was no point. It was an invalid argument after all. It didn't matter what his intentions had been; all that mattered was how it impacted this person who was so precious to him. "All right, I understand," Ansel said.

Sebastian paused, taking a breath. Ansel could feel the anxiety mounting in his voice over the phone. He knew Sebastian must be glad not to have to do this in person. Ansel himself wasn't so sure he would have had the strength for a face to face meeting. Sebastian was his haven in the woods. Whenever Ansel felt the loneliest, or the happiest, he knew he could always share that with Sebastian. Sebastian was always happy for his friends and actively made an effort not to judge them,a trait he and Ansel had in common.

Ansel may have been maddeningly indecisive, but he took time to listen and understand people. He made it so that to be in his presence, in close range of his chestnut brown eyes, meant being in a flow of freedom and comfort. As a result of his charming nature, Ansel was not usually met with resistance when we wanted someone, except for now with Sebastian.

"I love you, Ansel, but I also feel like I'm addicted to you. I need to value myself first," Sebastian said. "You are my best friend, but if we keep crossing the line emotionally, we'll lose each other."

Ansel felt those words nick at his bones. Sebastian was right. The first time they'd had sex in Philadelphia it had just happened. They were out on the town and with a pretty girl. They were drunk and let their curiosities take them. But following their encounter, they couldn't deny things had changed between them. They had seen each other either half-dressed or fully nude a million times before, but when your lips are meeting and your fingertips are rushing all over each other's bodies, it's a lot different.

The second time they'd had sex, it was because they wanted to; it was to say goodbye. They missed each other and they had acknowledged being attracted to each other, and that was supposed to be the last time they saw each other. Ansel called Sebastian, broke the silence, the wave he was supposed to ride out of town on. Nothing happened sexually; he just went over to talk about Isabelle. Ansel understood exactly why Sebastian didn't want to keep crossing the line. Twice was more than enough.

If it happened more than twice, it would keep happening for a while. They'd get lost in each other, until they couldn't find their way out. He knew how he felt about Sebastian, but he also knew that Sebastian was right. Ansel wasn't sure of what he wanted. He couldn't say he wanted a relationship. He didn't want to commit to staying in Hunter. Yet, he couldn't say he didn't want a relationship. Sebastian was his best friend, and it would be so amazing to date him. And it wasn't fair to leave Sebastian in limbo, while he tried to figure it all out. Ansel stood there in the dark, realizing this was the end of something more than friendship between them. There was silence on the phone for a long while. Ansel wished that he could be there to hold Sebastian, but he knew it would not make things any better.

Sebastian broke the silence. "I'm sure you need some time to process this. We'll talk again soon, okay?"

"Okay," Ansel said. He stood there for a minute, unable to move. When he gathered his strength, he found himself sitting distraught in front of the glass sliding door.

Chapter Sixteen

A week passed and Ansel hardly remembered anything. The days were a blur of booze and flashing lights. The binge had begun the day after his talk with Sebastian. He had thrown himself into the city's sparse nightlife in the hope of distracting himself from the pain he was feeling, but it hadn't worked. It hurt him immensely to stand there and do nothing, as his best chance for love escaped him. He remembered thinking that it felt as if his heart was actually broken, that it might give in and stop beating out of agony.

Despite this, Ansel knew that he had to continue on the path he had chosen. The decision was made. It was what was best for both of them. He was in no shape to take on anything serious. He had turned twenty-one and slept with his best friend in the spring. Just a few short months later, he had witnessed his grandfather's burial and the long-delayed dissolution of his immediate family just a week earlier, and he was still coming to grips with it. Add in having sex with your best friend, for a second time, and you're bound for an emotional breakdown.

He could have seen it coming, perhaps prevented it, but it was too late. As if losing his granddad and watching his family fall apart weren't enough, his ordeal with Sebastian was there to reiterate that sometimes it really is too late in life to take certain steps. It was the first real instance in which he felt completely powerless. Up until that moment, Ansel had lived a life that allowed him to make up for his mistakes. When he missed a test in high school, he knew he could make it up the next day at lunch. During his first two years at Walden, he would miss class altogether, and make it up on exams.

He was constantly finding excuses to reschedule appointments, and nobody questioned it. He developed the habit after his mom placed him in therapy. He had attended therapy twice weekly for all four years of high school. Once it was over, it was like he couldn't bring himself to set another schedule. His whole life had been routine—psychiatrist twice weekly, school Monday through Friday, piano every other Saturday until he quit at fifteen.

He felt so controlled, so restricted. When he finally had freedom, he ran all the way to Philadelphia with it. Even after moving to Philly, he had kept one foot in the world at home. That was over now. His family was going to sell the house. His mom would probably travel, and his sisters would retreat to their corners of the earth. His hometown friends were going on with their lives. His friends in Philly were going to graduate. That was that.

He had wasted so much time stuck in his own head that he'd failed to see it. He was tired of spending time any other way than how he wanted to. After falling apart on Luca and Isabelle's living room floor, he made up his mind that he was going to start living. In just one week, he had partied his way across town. There were only four bars in Hunter: Seven, Russo's, Crate, and the Kenwick, so this was a rather effortless task.

On Monday, he had margaritas at Seven. Tuesday, he went to Russo's for tacos and tequila. Wednesday, he rested at Isabelle's, and Thursday, he quenched his thirst at Crate. Luca had joined him at the Kenwick on Friday, for half-priced whiskey Cokes. The Kenwick was rather large for a bar. It was two stories high, painted black, had a giant oak door and glowing white neon sign overhead. The top floor boasted two foosball machines, a small seating area, a half bar, and a pool table.

The ground floor contained a larger seating area, full bar, and several more pool tables, as well as a connecting patio located at the back of the building. The basement doubled as a nightclub. Ansel and Luca were seated on the ground floor, by one of the large swing windows, facing the front of the bar. Luca had come out to get his mind off of Ari, who was set to be leaving for Florida the next morning. After their first drinks were served, Luca opened up.

Apparently, Ari had convinced his parents not to send him to rehab. Instead, he asked to stay with his uncle in Tampa. This uncle was supposed to live in some remote area, where there'll be no trouble for Ari to get into. The Beckmans were hoping the time alone would straighten him.

"Straighten like 'straighten' or rid him of his cocaine dependency?" Ansel asked.

"The latter. He hasn't told them he's gay yet."

Ansel understood. It wasn't like Ari could freely tell his parents he was gay on top of dealing with a drug addiction. That was going to take time. "So, is he your boyfriend now or what?" Ansel said, grinning. A second whiskey Coke arrived at the table for each of them.

"Well, not officially." Luca said, flushed. He finished his first drink, and Ansel emptied his glass as well. "Anyway, I haven't told my parents yet either, since they're still on vacation. I don't know what my dad will say, but I know my mom will probably ask if I'm seeing anyone. I kind of want to wait until Ari gets home, so he can be there."

"Damn, you two are getting serious, huh?"

"Not exactly, but I have known him since high school, and you know how my parents are. They want to meet everyone."

Ansel chuckled. A mixture of excitement and heartbreak swept across Luca's face, and Ansel knew why. He did indeed know how Luca's parents were. They were quiet people, stern disciplinarians, and full of traditional values. They were going to have enough trouble accepting their son's sexuality as it was; adding a character like Ari to the mix wasn't going to make it any easier.

"I just don't want them to think he's an entitled brat who can't function in the real world," Luca said after a long silence. "Because he's not; he's great. He just needs a little help."

"A little love?" Ansel said.

"And I'm the cheesy one in the group?" Luca said.

Ansel chuckled again. They finished their second drinks and ordered another round. After the fourth round they ordered whiskey neats. After their fifth round, Ansel stopped, but Luca kept drinking. The music roared in through the speakers mounted on the walls, far above their heads. The music made them want to dance, so they stumbled downstairs to the basement. Feeling the spirit of the alcohol running through their veins, they danced wildly to several songs, before Luca grew upset.

"I need to get out of here. I need to see Ari," he slurred.

"Okay, but neither of us should be driving." Ansel said. He began to call a ridesharing service, but Luca stopped him, insisting Ari could pick them up instead. Ansel flashed his friend a lukewarm smile. "You go ahead," he said. "I'll call a ride. I don't want to be a third wheel."

"Come onnnnn," Luca said, tugging on Ansel's sleeve. Before Ansel effectively protested, Luca had already stepped into a quiet corner of the room to make the call. Ari arrived approximately thirty-five minutes later, in his candy-apple-red sixty-nine Ford Mustang. He insisted that Ansel would not be a third wheel.

"You haven't...you're not drinking, right, Ari?" Luca said.

"No, surprisingly, I'm deathly sober," Ari said.

The ride was quiet and scenic from then on. Ansel had actually begun to sober up on the way, the cool night breeze caressing his skin. Within a few blocks, he realized that they had missed the turn to drop him off. "Hey, I'm staying on Rosewood Avenue," he said.

"Well, I figured it's extremely late, and you can crash at my place," Ari said.

Ansel checked his phone for the time and saw that it was somehow 3:00 a.m. already. He did not protest, as he would have to wake Isabelle to get in. He took a nap and a short while later awoke in the Beckmans' driveway. Dizziness still overcame him, but he didn't feel as inebriated as he had previously. The three young men exited Ari's Mustang and made their way down the winding brick pathway to the house. Ansel remembered entering and feeling it empty for the first time. Furniture and ornate decorations he surmised must have been hidden away during parties filled every corner, but it was still somehow empty. It was a sweeping mansion filled with nothingness. Suddenly Ansel began to feel an ounce of what he imagined Ari and Ally must've experienced there all the time. It was akin to his relationship with his family's old colonial.

"Feel free to crash in one of the guest rooms. There's quite a few, so you can take your pick. If you need anything, just shout. If I don't hear you, a member of the staff will," Ari said. He walked into the kitchen and grabbed a bottle of gin out of the cupboard.

"I think he's had enough," Ansel said, pointing to Luca.

"Oh, don't worry, this is for me," Ari said, winking.

"Baby needs to catch up," Luca yelled, slapping Ari's ass.

With that, Ari and Luca stumbled off into the darkness, presumably to Ari's room. Ansel walked over to the countertop in the far corner of the kitchen and poured himself a glass of water. He drank half of it and sat up on the countertop, gazing out into the space in front of them.

He heard a voice say, "What the hell do you think you're doing?"

Ansel recognized it was Ally immediately. She came in through the side entrance to the kitchen and glowered at him for a moment. As the tension between them heightened, she laughed and conceded that she was kidding. She had given Ansel a good fright, though he did not dare admit it. She walked over to him, put her hands on the counter next to his, and asked him how sober he was.

"Pretty damn sober now, I hate to admit," Ansel said.

"Good. I can do this," she said, leaned in, and kissed his lips. She ran her hands up his waist and walked in closer, until she was standing right between his legs. She had taken control, and he had succumbed without hesitation. Her lips tasted like melodies. Her skin against his felt like waves crashing against the shore in the summer. She bled into his body through her kiss and fed him with the vibrations of her touch.

She pulled him in extremely close, ran her hand up his shirt to feel his torso. He was fit. He was happy he was able to offer that. She peeled his shirt back with her other hand and broke their kiss. She stared him straight in the eyes, while running her free hand across his exposed torso. She urged him down from the counter and led him into her bedroom. He remembered kicking his shoes off at her bedroom door.

The feeling of the plush carpet, the soothing lavender-colored bedroom walls around him, and the electricity of her body against his returned to him once more. That night, she consumed him, on that lovely plush carpet of her bedroom floor. He awoke the next morning, recalling how she had exhausted him. There was a stinging pain running down the length of his back. When she sprung awake beside him, she looked into his eyes, still glowing, ethereal.

"I want you to know that this meant nothing. You're cute, I think you're cool, and I might call you again—but this meant nothing."

"Got it," he replied. He was not disappointed. He didn't have anything to offer her anyway. Besides, his heart was still very much with Sebastian. Yet, he couldn't ever actually have Sebastian. He had to come up with a game plan. And now he had discovered he lacked the strength to resist Ally Beckman. Normally, these troubles would have drowned him, but he had been neck-deep in the water for so long that it no longer fazed him.

After confirming they had an understanding, Ally pulled out her bong and packed it. They smoked for approximately fifteen minutes before Ari came knocking on the door and inquired as to whether Ansel was there. Ally affirmed that he was, unabashed.

"Well, quit getting him stoned. I need to take Luca home, if I'm going to make my flight."

"Fine," Ally huffed. She passed Ansel the bong once more.

He took another hit. "I'll meet you guys outside."

She brushed her hand over his chest and up the back of his neck, causing him instant chills. He stared into her eyes again and felt his legs becoming liquid.

"I should get going." He rose, finished dressing, and exited the room. By the time he got out to the driveway, he found Ari and Luca already waiting in Ari's car for him. "Sorry," he said briefly and got into Ari's Mustang. They drove in silence, but it was not an overbearing, awkward silence, just the calm quiet of dawn. The sun's rays came in soft and subtle through the cloudy summer sky. When they reached Luca and Isabelle's place, Luca got out of the car as well. They stood there, away from the car, but still in front of the building for a moment. Meanwhile Ari lit and smoked a cigarette.

"So, you and Ally, huh?"

"It's not like that," Ansel said. "We're friends."

"The bite marks on your neck seem to disagree," Luca retorted.

Ansel chuckled. The two friends hugged, and Ansel winced a bit as Luca's hand brushed across his back. Luca didn't notice and walked toward Ari's car. When Luca arrived at the passenger side door, he fixed his eyes on Ansel and smiled. "Here I was hoping we'd double date."

Ansel shrugged him off, waved goodbye to Ari, and made his way into the copper-colored high rise. He rode the elevator to the fifth floor and knocked quietly but assertively on Isabelle's door. Isabelle answered in a flowing red silk robe and matching pajama set. She ushered him inside and asked what happened to his neck. He claimed spiders were the culprit.

"Right," she said in a tone dripping with utter disbelief. "Well, I'm going back to bed," she added and waltzed out of the room.

Once inside, he walked himself to the guest bathroom. His curiosity at the source of the pain emitting from his back had piqued He pulled up his shirt and turned his neck to look over his left shoulder. He saw long thin scratches running up and down the length of his spine. He sighed a sigh of relief, remembering how he had gotten them. Ally Beckman.

The Nabokov quote instantly surfaced in his mind: *she was exasperation, she was torture.* He walked out of the bathroom and lay down on the sofa in the living room. He blinked at the ceiling a few times and fell asleep. He awoke in the afternoon realizing that he had run out of bars in the city to visit. Luca opted to stay inside. He was still coping with the fact that Ari had gone to Florida. This left Ansel and Luca to buy a bottle of rum and finish it with Isabelle at the apartment.

By Sunday morning, Ansel had convinced Luca to come out for mimosas with everyone at the Jazz Club, a local restaurant that only featured local jazz players. They had breakfast, drank their mimosas, and updated one another on the details of their lives.

Chapter Seventeen

Another week passed and Ansel continued drowning his sorrows. On Monday, he went to a party with Luca on the north side of town, near the border with Riverton. On Tuesday, he went to two different parties near Hunter Community College, one of which Ally attended. The two ended up hooking up there and retiring to her place. By Wednesday, he had made it into Riverton and swept through their dive bars. He visited six bars in total on that night.

He went on to hit four more on Thursday. On Friday after just two drop-ins, he wound up at Ally's for another night of pure exasperation. It was Saturday, June 27, when Ansel awoke with a pounding headache on Luca and Isabelle's living room floor. He was still dressed in his clothes from the night before. He could not bring himself to move. The blinding misery between his temples paralyzed him. He took a deep breath in the hope of easing his suffering. It did not help.

He found his throat as dry as though he had spent several years stranded in the desert. He knew he had to get up to get water, but even just thinking about moving hurt. After lying there on his back for several minutes, he finally mustered up the courage to roll onto his stomach and get up on his knees. He shook like a fawn learning to walk for the first time. He stalled on his knees, before once again mustering up enough strength to rise to his feet. Once he was on his feet, the pounding in his temples only intensified. He eased his way to the kitchen and poured himself a glass of filtered water. He must not have been as quiet as he had imagined, because Isabelle had come out of her room to investigate.

"Oh, it's just you."

"Sorry about the racket."

"No worries. Let me get you some ibuprofen."

"Thanks," Ansel said. Due to all the drinking he had done, his throat was incredibly dry, and his voice came out sounding raspy, like an old jazz singer.

Isabelle left the room, returned with two reddish-brown pills, and handed them to Ansel. Ansel swallowed them with much haste and collapsed against the refrigerator. Though he drank a considerable amount of water, the metallic taste of the ibuprofen lingered in his mouth. He asked her what time it was.

Isabelle studied the clock on the microwave. "Eleven forty-five." Ansel grunted a thank-you. "You know you can't go on like this, right?"

"Like what?" Ansel strained through a tired and raspy voice.

Isabelle refused to capitulate. "You know what I'm talking about."

He didn't argue. He didn't have the strength to argue with her, and she was right anyhow. "I know, just hurts less this way."

Isabelle turned to him and asked what he was accomplishing by getting hammered every night and sleeping with Ally Beckman. He couldn't answer her. He didn't know. There was no point to his excessive drinking or getting entangled with Ally, and that had become the point in a way. He was rebelling for the sake of rebelling against his family, himself. He had long been the awkward, queer kid, and now he had finally begun to bloom. He wasn't going to get over his feelings for Sebastian by partying them away, but the late nights provided a distraction from the confusion gripping him. Ansel slumped on Isabelle's sofa and the intercom in her apartment rang.

"I have a surprise for you," she said to Ansel. Isabelle pressed the buzzer, and a moment or so later, there was a knock at the door. She went to answer and Sebastian walked in behind her. Ansel thought he would collapse, partially from shock and partially from the massive hangover he was suffering with.

"You reek," Sebastian said, and sat down on the sofa beside Ansel.

"Thanks."

"I'll give you two some privacy," Isabelle whispered before leaving the room once more.

Once she was safely out of the room, Sebastian spoke, "You're going to damage your liver, your kidneys, or worse if you keep this up."

Ansel tried defending his behavior. "I've been having fun for a couple of weeks, no big deal. Why are you here?" He pivoted. He had not expected to see Sebastian so soon, given the way their last conversation had ended.

"I still need space, but I care about you. We're friends above all else, and I deeply regret our last talk closing on such a tenuous note."

Hi pleas were ill received, and Ansel cut him off midstream. Ansel's eyes had welled up. Sebastian loved him, but Ansel was fully cognizant that he had proven himself to be indecisive and unreliable. He would be selfish to expect Sebastian to help him sort through any more emotional baggage.

"Look, I'm trying to stop you from making a huge mistake," Sebastian said. "Sure, you're having fun now getting wasted and taking comfort in Ally Beckman, but what happens when that ends?"

"I don't know, and how do you know about Ally?" Ansel asked. He was practically certain that none of their close mutual friends had said anything, and he was right.

"One of my classmates at Hunter Community saw you two hooking up at a party."

"Are you bothered?" Ansel said. He desperately wanted to know, as if it would help him gauge the depth of Sebastian's affection for him, validate it more even.

"Believe it or not, no," Sebastian said, strolling beside him. "I'm not going to lie, I was hurt at first, but I know that it's just sex and that you're acting out of pain." Ansel ached to say something, but feared he'd choose the wrong words, so he remained silent. Sebastian continued, "I understand how you feel. I just don't want to see you spiral."

Ansel took a breath and managed to speak. "I appreciate the concern, but this isn't all because of what happened between us."

"I know that too. It has more to do with you losing your granddad, the subsequent drama with your family, and the fear you must be feeling about what comes next. The reality is you are the only one in charge of your destiny. As Maya Angelou once said, 'You cannot control all the events that happen to you, but you can decide not to be reduced by them.'"

"I never knew you read Maya Angelou. I'll stay in tonight."

"Good, and so you know, you haven't lost me. I just need more time before I can put what's happened behind me."

"All right."

With that, Sebastian rose and gave Ansel a friendly hug. He walked out of the apartment. Ansel sat there slumped on the sofa and stared up at the ceiling once more. His eyes flickered a bit and felt his temples relax. *The ibuprofen must be kicking in*, he thought. His eyes flickered again, and he felt his pulse slow. He turned over on his side and fell asleep. When he awoke again, the sun had already begun to set. He walked over to the sliding door that led to the balcony. He slid the door and the adjoining screen open a pinch and leaned halfway outside. He stared at the city through the screen. He thought about everything that had transpired that summer. The shiny steel and tempered glass windows of skyscrapers downtown twinkled, as the last light of day fell upon them.

Chapter Eighteen

The end of her cigarette burned slow and steady in the evening air. Regina exhaled deeply, putting the butt out on the brick wall behind her. She waved away the lingering smoke and spritzed herself with body spray. She walked out from the parking lot and down West Sixth Street to the large stone building with Splash written in big, bold, bright red letters on the front of it. *Splash*, Regina thought to herself, *what a stupid name for an art gallery.*

It seemed all the galleries in Downtown LA had to have some kitschy name. Regina strutted inside, in her black off-the-shoulder Christian Dior dress. She shook hands with her agent and went to work the room. The crowd was in awe of her as usual. The event photographers asked her to pose next to the placards with her name on them, as usual. Potential buyers all wanted to meet her and get a picture with her as well.

She signed postcards with reproductions of her paintings on them. She smiled and waved to people she hardly liked. The whole thing had become so dreary to her. Just as she was receiving praise for her bas-relief work from some pompous magazine editor, she spotted her sister

Elise out of the corner of her eye. She grabbed a champagne flute off a tray, held by one of the cater waiters, downed the contents, and walked over to Elise calmly. The stinging to her cheek had long subsided, but the memory still pulsed on in her mind. "I wasn't expecting to see you here," Regina said, handing the empty flute off to another waiter.

"I wasn't planning on coming," Elise said, "but I changed my mind last minute."

"How generous of you," Regina replied, her voice soaked in sarcasm.

"Listen, despite what happened, you're still my sister, and I still care about you. You were right. I was kind of jealous. I mean, it's not like he and I ever spent any time together, outside of rehearsals. He probably never knew I was attracted to him. Anyway, I should have never let a man come between us, and I'm sorry for slapping you at dinner."

Although she tried her hardest to remain upset, Regina couldn't help but soften. She reached her arms out and hugged her sister. It was not for show, not because they had an audience—it was a genuine, heartfelt embrace.

"I'm sorry I hurt you," Regina said. It was the first instance in a long time that Regina had apologized for anything and meant it.

"Want to go get something to eat?" Elise asked. "A cute French bistro recently opened up on Seventh Street."

"God, yes," Regina replied. Although she had only been at Splash for fifteen minutes, Regina walked out of the gallery arm in arm with her sister.

Chapter Nineteen

It was Tuesday, June 30, when Ansel received the news. He was on a hike at John Muir Memorial Park at the time. It felt surreal. A sinking feeling washed over him. The news came in the form of a call from Luca. Ansel couldn't make out what was going on at first. There were only inaudible noises on the other end. As the noises continued, Ansel perceived them to be some sort of screeching. He realized it was sobbing, deep, woeful sobbing.

He hurried down from the hillside, in the hopes that his cell signal would improve. Once the line was clearer, Ansel heard Luca shout, "Ari's dead, he's dead!" in between loud sobs. Ansel asked Luca to calm down and promised to meet him. The call got disconnected. Ansel almost dropped his phone as he rushed down the hillside. He managed to call a ridesharing service and raced to meet his ride at the entrance to the park.

Ansel heeded the panic in Luca's voice ringing out in his head and knew he had to get to Luca's place right away. After weaving in and out of traffic, the rideshare driver finally arrived at Luca's house. Ansel hurried out of the car and knocked on the door rapidly, but no one answered. There were no other cars in the driveway, and no sounds emitting from the front of the house. Ansel went around the rear of the house. Once in Luca's backyard, he lifted the large potted eucalyptus to reveal the family's spare key.

He entered the house and called for Luca, when a loud crash came booming from upstairs. He ran up to Luca's room and opened the door to discover his friend sitting on the floor sobbing heavily. As Ansel approached, Luca abruptly got up and threw his computer chair at the wall on the other end of the room. Loose pieces of plaster jettisoned to the floor. He curled into a fetal position on the floor.

"Luca, stop and breathe," Ansel said. "Look at me, you're going to be all right, breathe."

Luca flailed and pointed to his dresser. Ansel knew exactly what he was referencing. He went over to the dresser and found Luca's inhaler in the second drawer from the top. He brought it over to Luca, who pumped and inhaled deeply.

"What happened?" Ansel said while rubbing his friend's back.

"He was involved in some sort of drag racing acci-dent. The car flipped and went up in flames. He was pro-nounced dead at the scene," Luca managed through a heavy stream of tears. Ansel embraced his friend and sat with him until the tears subsided.

"When do your parents get home?" Ansel asked as Luca sniffled.

"Friday," Luca said. He turned to Ansel, still teary-eyed. "Will you stay the night?"

"Of course," Ansel said. It occurred to him to ask about Ally. She wasn't just Ari's sister. She was his twin after all. "Does Ally know?" Ansel asked.

"She's the one who told me," Luca said.

She must be absolutely devastated, Ansel thought. He had lost his father and grandfather, but he couldn't imagine what it must feel like to lose someone you'd come into the world with. With Luca's permission, Ansel excused himself to go call Ally. He scaled the stairs and ventured out to the backyard. His head was spinning, and for the first time in weeks, it was not due to alcohol. Ally answered after the fourth ring. Her voice was worn and monotone like someone who had been crying nonstop.

"How are you?"

"I don't know. It feels like part of me vanished when Ari died."

"I can come see you,"

"No, it's fine. I need some time to myself."

If anyone appreciated the desire to be left alone after such an important loss, it was Ansel. "I understand."

"Thanks for checking in though, I really appreciate it."

Ansel didn't feel much relief after ending the call. He returned to Luca's room trying desperately to conceal his discouragement.

"So will you be taking off to be with Ally?"

"Well I wasn't going to leave right now regardless of the outcome of the call, but nah I asked if she wanted me to come see her and she declined, which I totally get." Ansel walked over to Luca, who was now seated on his bed, and sat beside him.

They stayed there in silence for some time, before Ansel got the idea to put on some music to help ease things. He selected random play on Luca's computer, and Milky Chance's "Sweet Sun" played. Ansel returned to his spot next to Luca and placed his arms around his friend. He held Luca as he sobbed, and the song played on. Luca hardly spoke the rest of the evening. He would begin a sentence and begin to cry again.

Nothing came out clearly. He had lost someone he had grown to care for so much. He had never known loss before. He had never grieved for a loved one. He had been lucky until now. Eventually, Luca grew tired, and Ansel set up camp on the bedroom floor with spare blankets they found in the closet in the hall. The room was quiet. Both boys had closed their eyes and drifted off to sleep. Around 3:30 a.m., Ansel awoke to Luca gasping for air. Ansel grabbed the inhaler and handed it to Luca. He left the room and reentered with a tall glass of water that he handed to Luca as well.

"It's okay. Breathe," Ansel said, rubbing Luca's shoulders as Luca pumped his inhaler. "Do you want to talk about it?"

"I kept seeing Ari's face. He was staring straight at me and screaming for help. I can still see his eyes, those beautiful green eyes weeping—begging someone to save him," Luca said, breathing a bit steadier, but still shaking.

Ansel blinked for a moment, and he could see those same eyes staring at him. Ally's eyes. "It's going to be okay. You're going to be okay," Ansel assured him.

"Smoke with me?"

"Top drawer of your dresser?"

"Yep."

Ansel walked over to the cherry wood dresser, making sure to step over Luca carefully. Luca sat up. Ansel turned the ceiling fan on low and opened the window at the far corner of the room. Ansel went over to Luca's bed and sat at the edge of it. Ansel handed Luca the blue-and-yellow pipe and the baggie that had been lying next to it in the top dresser drawer.

Luca packed and lit the pipe and inhaled deeply. The thick cannabis smoke was swished around the room, and out through the window by way of the ceiling fan. They sat there taking turns smoking for about ten minutes. Ansel suggested they practice a meditation exercise he'd learned back in Philly. Luca shrugged and gave it a try. He inhaled deeply and Ansel guided them with positive affirmations. *Inhale strength, exhale doubt. Inhale healing, exhale pain. Inhale light, exhale darkness.*

Chapter Twenty

Luca arose the next morning to typing. He sat up in his bed, wiped the sleep from his eyes, and discovered Ansel seated at his computer clicking away at the keyboard. Ansel rocked back and forth a bit in the slightly dented chair as he worked. Luca, hoarse from all the crying he had done the night before, strained to ask what his friend was up to. Ansel smiled coyly and said job hunting. He had applied to several coffee shops and a neon museum set to open in downtown next month. Luca didn't say anything. He simply got up, walked over to Ansel, and hugged him. A wide grin swept across Ansel's face.

"You know you can always stay here if you need a place, right?" Luca said. "My parents adore you anyway."

"I know," Ansel said, "and thanks, but I couldn't do that to you right now."

Luca merely nodded, knowing his friend didn't want to overwhelm him. He peered over at the corner of the room, where he had thrown the chair the night before. The wall retained a considerable crack, but all the miniscule pieces of plaster had been cleaned up.

Noticing where Luca's eyes had wandered, Ansel noted, "I grabbed the hand-vac and cleaned it up. I figured it would help a bit."

"Nothing a giant poster can't fix," Luca said. He laughed for the first time in twenty-four hours, and a wave of relief fell over the room. Ansel asked if his nightmare had returned. "No, but I still didn't sleep well," Luca said. "Medicating last night helped though. Honestly having you here helped."

"Well, if you'd rather not be alone, I can stay until your parents get back," Ansel said.

"That would be great," Luca replied.

The two went downstairs, and each poured themselves a bowl of cereal. Luca took a shower and called out of work. Ansel and Luca spent the rest of the morning watching *Avatar: The Last Airbender*. Ansel assessed Luca every so often, and noticed he was occasionally in tears. They spent the early afternoon in Luca's backyard meditating and talking. A serious conversation arose while they sat cross-legged on the grass. The warmth of the summer sun on their backs soothed them as they spoke.

"I'm okay until Ari crosses my mind. It's like there's a half-working levee inside me. Sometimes it does its job, and I feel in control. Other times, the levees rupture, and everything comes flooding out," Luca said.

"You're probably going to feel like that for a while. I felt the same way when my dad passed, and again with my granddad. The biggest lie anyone will tell you is the pain will go away. It won't. You will hurt every time you think about it, but you will hurt less as each day goes by. You will never be completely prepared to deal with someone's death, but at least now you will know what to expect."

"Gee, thanks," Luca said.

Ansel apologized, sensing the sarcasm in Luca's tone. Luca waved off the apology and genuinely thanked his friend for being honest. "You're welcome, jerk," Ansel replied and nudged his friend in the rib. They took in deep breaths, inhaling the scent of the earth beneath them. Three house sparrows flew by in trapeze-like formations, before whirling away from the whirring breeze. They went back inside as the breeze picked up. Isabelle came over that evening after she got off from work. The three watched a movie together. They chose a cheesy, older, action flick, so they could make fun of the effects. They laughed into the night until they all grew tired. Luca awoke twice that night, once out of breath, the second time screaming. Ansel sprang into action both times, with reassuring words and Luca's inhaler.

"It was his eyes again, those eyes," he said to Ansel, crying.

"I know. Breathe, buddy. You are going to be all right. Breathe," Ansel said, lulling his friend to sleep. Luca's parents returned home from their vacation two evenings later. They entered the living room to find their son and Ansel seated, patiently waiting for them. Luca explained how their friend Ari had passed away. His parents immediately got up to hug him. Before they got close enough to touch him, Luca advised that they should both remain seated. He went on to explain how Ari had become more than a friend.

He confessed to his parents that he was bisexual, and that Ari was his lover. His parents didn't know what to do or say at first. His mother got up and hugged him. His father followed suit. They both apologized for the loss he must be feeling and told Luca they loved him. Ansel let out a deep sigh of relief. He hugged Luca, bid Luca's parents farewell, and left. As he strolled down the street, his mind strayed to how his own coming out had been so much tenser. He was happy that Luca did not have to endure that, while coping with the loss of someone he cared for. Ansel walked down Valley Way and wound up on Avery Boulevard. He waited by the bus stop. He gazed up at the sky, engrossed in the swirls of lavender and ochre orangish light. The sun descended beneath the horizon, and the month of June came to a quiet end.

Chapter Twenty-One

They say the eyes are the windows to the soul. It is practically impossible not to believe that is true. After all, one can decipher love, anguish, truth, and dishonesty, all from peering into someone's eyes. Not only that, but when the eyes are closed, the world inside your mind opens up through dreams. Ansel closed his eyes and was presented with a clear vision of his mother's eyes staring at him. Those eyes chock-full of disapproval, disappointment, sadness, love. He saw the heartbreak in Sebastian's eyes.

He blinked his eyes open again and saw those effervescent green eyes of Ally's. They were the same eyes as her brother's. The same eyes that Luca saw pleading with him in his nightmares. Ansel blinked again, and a sea of red swept in, in waves. The fleshy, telltale red that marks the inside of one's eyelids. Ansel's soft chestnut eyes fluttered open, and the red sea ebbed.

Ansel was alone in the forest of hills that rose above the town of Hunter, California. He was seated cross-legged on the dry earth. His feet were exposed to the harsh wind and sunlight. He soaked in his surroundings with each breath. Mr. and Mrs. Beckman had their son cremated. Ally suggested it. They were incapable of bringing themselves to selecting a coffin for him. His body had been severely burned as a result of the accident as well. In fact, their uncle in Tampa was hardly able to identify Ari when he arrived at the scene. The coroner had to use dental records to confirm Ari's identity.

They held a memorial service for Ari on Saturday, July 3. Luca remarked on the next day there'd be fireworks for Ari. Three weeks had since passed. Ansel had officially begun living with Isabelle. With Holly's help, he had arranged to sublet his apartment in Philly until the lease expired. Holly had also shipped him his clothes. Meanwhile, Luca, expectedly, still was not himself; and almost no one heard a peep out of Ally.

At Ari's memorial service, she did her best to put on a kind face and give everyone warm-hearted thank-yous. There were at least fifty uninvited guests that showed up to pay their respects. They were all well aware some of the mourners hardly even knew Ari; but all were welcomed regardless. They were friends of friends at the least, and Ari would have wanted them there. Ansel remembered how Ally made it a point to hug everyone as they left, and how long she'd held on to Luca. She had been wearing the pendant of Saint Christopher that Luca had given her brother.

Since he couldn't bring himself to ask Ally how she got the pendant directly, Ansel did the next best thing and went to Isabelle.

"Her uncle in Tampa found it at the scene and brought it with him to give to her. During the crash, the necklace had been expelled far enough away from the car to evade melting in the blaze. The medical examiner determined that it must have been wrapped around Ari's fist at the time of impact. Ally discovered it was Luca's at the service. She tried to return it to him, but you know Luca, he insisted she keep it."

Three weeks passed, and Ansel still couldn't wrap his head around all of it. He had, however, become employed within that span of time. He received the call for an interview two days after Ari was memorialized. He put on the same dress shirt and slacks that he had worn two days earlier and for his granddad's funeral. He accented it with a black tie he had borrowed from Luca and made his way across town to meet with the owner of an e-commerce company. After Ari's passing, Ansel resolved to stay in Hunter and take charge of his future. He was finished with planning for the short-term alone. He recognized the risks involved, but they were worth the potential payout.

Besides, he had to stay. He had to reciprocate the unconditional support his friends had given him. Isabelle and Luca were undergoing monumental changes in their lives. They needed him. They all needed one another. Moreover, Ansel needed to establish some stability in his life. He couldn't keep running away from conflict. It was time for a change.

He scoured the internet until he came across a position for a junior web administrator for an online retailer named Ellsworth Inc. He did some research and found out Ellsworth was a growing consumer electronics business. Naomi Ellsworth had founded it in the living room of her one-bedroom apartment. She had since moved on to leasing an office, in a quaint three-story building near the town's border with Riverton. Ansel figured he could finally put the computer science classes he'd taken at Walden to use. He was hired immediately after his interview ended.

When Ansel worked at Artist Etc., there were three other employees. At Ellsworth, he was one of seventeen. Within the first few days of getting this new job, Ansel learned he preferred working in an office setting, as opposed to on his feet all day.

"Your duties include creating and updating listings, keeping track of online inventory, ordering merchandise, monitoring the shipping, and some light photo editing. It's a relatively easy job," Ms. Ellsworth said to him when he started, "but it requires focus. If you let tasks slip, things have the potential to get hectic."

Ansel internalized his new employer's warning. "Understood," he'd shot back. He was determined to turn his life around.

Death had touched not one, but two different people in his life. Witnessing the passing of his granddad was one thing. His granddad had been getting older. He hadn't had much time left. Ansel had known he would go one day. However, the news of Ari's death shook Ansel. He didn't dare display it in front of Luca. Luca needed his support, his strength, and encouragement—but Ari's death really shook Ansel.

He and Ari were the exact same age. They grew up in the same town. Ari was not elderly. His time was not running out. He was full of youth and exuberance. He was beautiful, smart, and funny. Ari just made poor choices. Ansel meditated on this. He was one party invitation away from ending up like Ari.

He thought back to the memorial service. Ansel closed his eyes, and he could hear the clergyman. *We are gathered here to celebrate the life of Aris Fitzwarren Beckman.* He could see the unadulterated sorrow played out upon Mr. and Mrs. Beckman's faces. Worse still, with each flutter of those rich summertime pastures she called eyes, he could almost feel the despair Ally was in. She'd lost her twin brother, her best friend. She gave this eulogy that flooded every dry eye. She talked about how strange it felt to be without Ari for the first time in her life.

"We were conceived together. We came into the world together, graduated together, and now he's suddenly gone. I know it sounds foolish, but part of me keeps expecting him to show up and cheer me on from the sidelines. Ari was always there to encourage me..." she said, breaking into tears herself.

Ansel imagined the torment she must've felt. He could still hear the words tremble from her lips, toward the end of her speech. She was enduring one of the most excruciating losses there was—her brother and her best friend all in one. Ansel took a deep breath and returned to reality as he respired. It was Monday, July 25, and he was seated at his cubicle at work. He had decorated the walls with photographs of adventures with his friends and knickknacks he'd picked up over the years. The idea was to create a peaceful, positive space, despite the fact that it was a cubicle.

Seated there, pondering on all that had transpired since he had arrived in Hunter, Ansel realized it worked. He felt much more at ease in the confined space. In fact, he felt much more at ease working for Ellsworth in general than he had working at the gallery in Philadelphia. The workday came to an end, and Ansel clocked out. He said his goodbyes to his coworkers as well as his boss, Naomi, and made his way out of the building. As he reached the bus stop, he received a call from none other than Sebastian. They had seen each other and spoken briefly at Ari's service, but they both agreed it was not the right time or place for a personal discussion.

Ansel also wanted to allow Sebastian the space that he had asked for. He was undeniably happy that Sebastian had finally contacted him, but he didn't want to seem too eager. Ansel picked up the phone. He and Sebastian made casual arrangements to meet at the neon museum that had recently opened. They strolled through the museum together, passing a sea of brilliant, multicolored lights. They stopped when they came to an installation by Dan Flavin. They entered the gallery by themselves.

It was pitch-dark, except for Flavin's light piece. They stood taking it in, as Sebastian noted it was the first time they had been alone together in nearly a month. In true to form fashion, Ansel replied by reminding him that technically they were not alone, since other people were in the museum. Sebastian nudged him, as if to say *you know what I meant*, and they walked on.

Feeling his nerves tense up, Ansel pivoted to making conversation before he lost the capacity to say anything at all. "How have you been?" It was a rather simple question, but he really did want to know the answer.

"Oh, you know, I've been all right. I fucked someone."

"Oh," Ansel was taken aback and trying to mask it but wasn't sure what else to say. He was certain Sebastian's lover wasn't anyone he was familiar with, but curiosity got the better of him. "Who?" he posed, as if knowing this would somehow make the news easier to digest. He instantly regretted asking as Sebastian raved about meeting a twink while barhopping in Silver Lake. "So, are you and this twink involved now on some level?" Ansel pushed further. Although Sebastian pretended to share freely, Ansel distinctly got the impression certain details were being withheld. He had no right to be upset. Sebastian wasn't on trial, and Ansel wasn't his boyfriend. Yet Ansel's heart filled with the same vitriolic mix of jealousy and sadness known solely to spurned lovers.

"Nope, we fucked a few times though."

There was something about the way Sebastian said "fucked," a quality to it that was both painful and laissez-faire that stayed with Ansel. It hung in the air and rung out in his ears. "A few times, huh?" he said before asking what led to it. By the look on Sebastian's face, Ansel could tell their life-long roles were reversing. Sebastian was now the vulnerable one, the one who couldn't keep his cool despite his most desperate efforts.

"Anger and loneliness practically consumed me after discovering you slept with Ally. It was irrational but sleeping with a stranger felt like getting even."

Ansel reflected on this. "Well, we're definitely even now," he said. "I understand where you're coming from. I guess I had assumed you didn't care whom I slept with."

"I care," Sebastian clarified, "but I didn't want to make a big deal out of it all." They strolled along side by side and tried to determine what would happen next. As they progressed, Ansel noticed Sebastian didn't turn to look at him while they spoke. Sebastian usually reveled in making eye contact. *He must be nervous*, Ansel reasoned. Eventually, Sebastian conceded that he was indeed brimming with apprehension. "I'm overcome by nerves I suppose. I hadn't planned this far ahead. I figured I would call you, we'd hang out, and I'd confess everything. Up until this point, my sole goal had been to see if there was any vestige of emotion in your eyes once you learned the truth."

"And?"

"And all I got was a stupid 'we're even' instead," Sebastian said. His tone was whimsical, but there was more than a twinge of truth to the sentiment. Ansel responded with laughter. It arose out of a mixture of nerves and relief.

"Sorry to disappoint," he finally said. "Although I must admit, despite the fact that I'm not angry, or sad about it, I am kind of jealous."

They strolled around the gallery, and Sebastian's face became illuminated by glowing green and blue lights. He turned to Ansel and asked if he really meant it.

"Yeah," Ansel said. "I mean I understand it's illogical. It's not like we were ever together, and I know I did the exact same thing, but I can't help it."

They left the neon museum and wound up taking the bus uptown together. They got off in front of Muir Memorial Park and strolled around until they landed at the old colonial. A giant For Sale sign hung from a fine wooden post that stood out on the front lawn. "Is anyone home," Sebastian asked.

"No. My mom is vacationing in Cabo with my aunt Nell, and Elise and Regina flew back to New York together."

"So, the War of the Wallises is officially over?"

"More or less," Ansel confirmed. Ansel and Sebastian sat down on the front lawn together, the same way they used to do when they were in high school.

"Why did you get involved with Ally Beckman?" Sebastian asked suddenly and seemingly out of the blue.

"Being with her was freedom. She took complete control, and I found it exhilarating to relinquish my power like that. It was also entirely devoid of any real significance, so I never had to wonder what if or think about where we were headed."

"Is that what you liked about it?"

"I guess, but I also value the fact that we were honest with each other. We didn't make any excuses for what we were doing or why we were there. She was in it to feel some semblance of control. I was in it to feel something—pain, pleasure, anything."

"And with me?"

"It was...it is different with you. We haven't been honest with each other lately, but you mean everything to me."

"Ah." Sebastian reclined on the cool grass and stared up at the vast, open sky above. "I wish things could have been easier with us," he said after a moment or two of silence. "In what way?" Ansel asked, curiosity thumping hard and deep in his veins.

"I wish," Sebastian started softly, "we were strangers to each other for one."

"Why?"

"Because we could have fallen in love."

Ansel didn't immediately say anything. He simply nodded and joined Sebastian in reclining on the lawn. After a while Ansel spoke. "Maybe we're together in some parallel universe. One where I'm not so damaged and you're not so enamored with things that aren't good for you."

"You think you aren't good for me?"

"Good, good enough, take your pick." They lay there processing their feelings, present in the moment, listening to low chirping of crickets off in the distance. They spent the rest of the evening lying there, staring at the stars that lined the sky above the old colonial.

Chapter Twenty-Two

Isabelle sat beaming at the dinner table. Luca was seated next to her, and Ansel was seated directly across from them. They began forking at their food when conversation began. Luca thanked Isabelle for cooking, and Isabelle mentioned that Ansel helped immensely.

"So, where is everyone situated these days?" Luca asked.

"Well, I took the master bedroom. Ansel now resides in my old room," Isabelle said, taking a large bite of her food after she finished. Silence ensued, as the bunch began chewing their food. The first break she got Isabelle re-ignited the conversation. "What's new in your lives, boys?" she asked, smiling.

Ansel spoke first. "I'm in love with my new job. My boss is so easygoing. Other than that not much."

When it was Luca's turn to share, he shrugged, then forked his food morosely and mumbled "still trying to cope with what had happened to Ari." Ansel and Isabelle apologized almost in unison.

"Well, maybe this will cheer you up," Isabelle said. "I met a hot new guy recently, and I totally pegged him last night."

"You what?" Luca's mouth slid ajar, and the food he had been chewing almost fell out of it.

"She pegged him," Ansel repeated, while trying and failing to contain his roaring laughter at the words.

"Oh my God, I can see it now," Luca said, laughter practically bursting from him as well. "Thank you, Issy, that cheered me up," he said after catching his breath.

"What was it like?" Ansel said.

"There's nothing like hearing a grown man begging and moaning for more like a kitten in heat, while you're drilling deep inside of him," Isabelle said. Both young men gave her a knowing glance in response, and with that the group finished their meals. After dinner, Isabelle went off to her room to rest. Ansel and Luca stacked the dishwasher, went out for a walk. Evening dew fell on the bare flesh of their arms, as they strolled down Rosewood Avenue. The glow of the streetlights set the sidewalk ablaze. After several moments of silence, Ansel asked Luca how he'd been doing lately.

"I've been all right," Luca said. "Sometimes the sadness feels like a little too much to bear, but you guys, my family, and Ally have been amazing. What about you?"

"I'm all right too, can't complain," Ansel said.

Luca glanced over at Ansel and wasn't buying it. "How's everything with Sebastian?" he asked, careful not to press Ansel too hard.

"I don't know," Ansel said, sighing, "but I don't want to get into it."

"Why not?" Luca asked though he already had the answer. Ansel didn't want to overwhelm him. He was cautious that way when it came to his friends and their feelings. He had assessed the situation and deduced Luca couldn't possibly handle any more drama. He was only partially right though. Luca couldn't have handled more drama, if it was occurring in his own life, but it wasn't. Ansel was the one in hot water, and Luca craved a distraction from obsessing over Ari's death. "Actually, never mind why. Tell me what's going on with you," he urged.

"I know, but there are people dealing with poverty, war, and famine, and my biggest concern is a guy. It seems trivial, especially after everything you've been through."

"Ansel, stop," Luca said, visibly irritated. "Those things will unfortunately continue to go on in the world. We're talking about you right now."

"Okay, relax," Ansel said, letting out a nervous chuckle. "Sebastian and I went to that new neon museum the other day. We talked about us and everything else, but I'm not sure exactly where we stand. I can't explain it, but it felt like things were irrevocably different between us."

"I think it's obvious you two are in love. Why are you letting him slip through your fingers like this?"

"I don't know. Maybe I'm afraid. I'm afraid of losing him. My friends are more to me than just friends. You guys are my family. If things didn't work out with Sebastian romantically...I just couldn't stand to lose him."

"If this summer has taught me anything, it's that we'll all lose each other someday. You will never truly be able to enjoy life, if you let that stop you. If I could have Ari back..." Luca's voice trembled. He paused and took a deep breath. "If I could have him back, I wouldn't waste a second hesitating," he said.

"You're right," Ansel said. He realized that in getting his life together, he had neglected to see the bigger picture. Life wasn't worth living if it wasn't actually being lived. He stopped walking, turned to Luca, and hugged him tightly.

"Let me guess. You have to run off to go see Sebastian now?" Luca said, half-sarcastic.

"Nah, I'm here with you right now. I can always call him later," Ansel said. He hung an arm around Luca's shoulder as they paced along together.

"Who are you, and what have you done with Ansel Wallis?" Luca said in disbelief.

Ansel simply laughed and shrugged in response. They finished their walk around the block and made their way inside. Isabelle had already retired to her room for the night. Ansel took this as his opportunity to meet with Sebastian. He sent a text, and Sebastian agreed to join him at a nearby mini park. Hunter was filled with mini parks. They were compact oases built into various neighborhoods to provide a balance between nature and city life. Ansel took his messenger bag with him and went to the park early to wait for Sebastian. Sebastian arrived right on time. They sat directly opposite of each other on a bench near the edge of the park.

"I wasn't going to do this, but someone reminded me how important it is not to waste the time you have with the people that you love." Ansel dove into his messenger bag and pulled out a lengthy letter. "I wrote you this letter a couple weeks ago. I didn't send it at first. I presumed you needed space, and who sends a letter nowadays anyway, right? Anyway, up until now, I wasn't planning on ever showing them to you."

Sebastian paused, reviewed the letter. It was a nearly a full page.

"If you prefer, I can leave so you have time to read it and process everything."

"No, stay," Sebastian said. He read through each line carefully, as Ansel sat there quiet and anxious. Ansel had not expected Sebastian to ask him to stay. He fidgeted a bit during the course of the first reading. By the time Sebastian eyes wandered to the bottom of the letter, Ansel's nerves had begun to surface. He kept replaying the contents again and again in his head.

I know I've failed to say this to you, but you are one of the most amazing people I have ever known, the letter started. *The reason I've been so apprehensive with you is due to sheer and utter fear. I fear that I'll take a wonderful opportunity and ruin it. I fear that I don't know how to properly love anyone, and that at best we'll fall apart just like my parents did. Worse still, I fear I'll lose you. Yet already being without you feels far more agonizing than my fears. Being without you is like watching a vivid sunrise a thousand times, without understanding the notion of color. I have survived many tragedies in my life. One of the most painful has been to know the divine taste of your lips, and not be able to have it every hour of the day. I wish there was some way that I could overcome this fear, because the torment of my inaction has blinded me to all the colors of your sunrise. I don't know if you will ever see this letter. But if you do, I hope you can forgive me for being so stupid. The truth is I'm in love with you. I love you with all the marrow in my bones.*

Sebastian put the letter down and didn't say anything for a while. Ansel looked at him, looked away, and laughed a nervous laugh. He drummed his fingertips against his sides, falling into absolute panic, with every passing moment. Sebastian turned to Ansel and broke the silence.

"Did you mean what you said in this letter?"

"All of it."

By then, Ansel noticed Sebastian's fingers had begun to tremble in his lap. Ansel watched as Sebastian clasped his hands together tightly to try to control it but was unsuccessful in doing so. Sebastian, ever the epitome of cool, was losing his composure. He tried to hide his feelings again, by running a hand through his hair, but that attempt also failed miserably.

"I love you with all the marrow in my bones."

A single tear slid down Sebastian's face as Ansel's words hung in the air. He dabbed at his eye and said, "I love you too, Ansel, but I can't be with you. I got another letter that predates yours. I got accepted to Tufts."

"Oh. I didn't even know you had applied."

"No one did. I didn't mention it. I didn't think I would get in. Yet here we are."

"Well, that's great news. When did you get the letter?"

"Shortly after we stopped speaking the first time. I didn't know how to tell you, and things were so confusing between us. I leave in two days."

"Shit." It was all Ansel managed to say. It was over. He had finally put his feelings on the line, and while the effort was admired, he did not get his happy ending. He had waited too long. Sebastian loved him, but he could not turn down spending the rest of his college years at Tufts. Ansel couldn't even fathom asking him to. Ansel stood up.

At first, it felt like all the air had fled his lungs. He could feel his face growing warm with embarrassment, and his knees shaking. He turned away from Sebastian, hoping to gather himself in that moment of privacy. He was unable to. Sebastian rose, and he hugged Ansel. They stood there entwined, their souls trying to nurse the sadness in each other. Sebastian brushed his chin across Ansel's cheek. Ansel nuzzled his face into the side of Sebastian's neck. Tears flowed down the sides of both of their faces. With the arrival of those tears came the break in the embrace. Ansel smoothed his shirt and shook his head from side to side. Sebastian straightened his collar and ruffled his hair. They each wiped tears from their own eyes and took a deep breath. This was goodbye. It was that invaluable lesson repeating itself; sometimes it really is too late.

Ansel mourned this loss; the same way he had mourned all the other losses he had experienced that summer. The missed opportunity, the missed chance at love. He mourned well into fall. The leaves of the sycamore trees turned amber and gold and journeyed down from their branches. He would play "Martha My Dear," and he couldn't help but sob. It went on like that until winter. He never understood why, but the rain always cleansed everything. It rained heavily that winter. Though he was under the lull of sadness for all of autumn, he knew he had to get on with the rest of his life. He had to go to work, class; he had to keep making something of himself. The world outside was still full of people—jackets and umbrellas and extra sweaters getting pulled out, tucked on. As the choreographed dance continued, he knew, so must he.

Chapter Twenty-Three

The trees had come alive again. The branches that had been laid bare during the winter months now gave birth to spry, green little leaflets. The calendar read spring, but the weather disagreed. It was ridiculously hot out, except for in the evenings. There was hardly any rain to be seen. A slight wind had picked up and swept across the parking lot of the health food market where Ansel, Isabelle, and Luca sat in Luca's car. They were basking in the pleasant climate and smoking a freshly rolled joint.

Clouds of smoke enveloped them and blended into the air. Luca coughed after his third or fourth turn. He vowed no more. They all agreed to exit the car and headed for the market. Vivid hues of red, yellow, and orange shone wildly under the overhead lighting at the entrance. The smell of fresh citrus permeated the air, as they strolled through the organic produce section. Senses heightened, they were in awe of everything around them. Isabelle marveled at the mangoes and playfully tossed one from palm to palm.

Luca was enraptured with some honeydew slices that had been freshly cut for customer trials. Ansel, meanwhile, was duly distracted by the store manager, a gorgeous brunette a couple of inches shorter than him. She had honey-colored eyes, dark brown skin, and the warmest smile. He was nearly certain that he'd seen her in his Eastern Philosophy class at Hunter Community. He thought about approaching her and striking up conversation a thousand times, but he wasn't sure of what to say. He'd been out of practice when it came to romance.

Everything went grey after Sebastian left, which Ansel could only describe as living in a fog. That fog lasted for nearly six months. Ansel knew the world would not end if he could not be with Sebastian, but it still felt like it might. It helped that he had been separated from Sebastian before. He grew more in touch with things than he had ever been. He began adjusting to the light again. It wasn't meant to be. Eventually, Ansel settled on that idea, without the shrill pang that he'd once felt gnawing at his ribs.

It was Sebastian's leaving that had encouraged Ansel to reenroll in school in the first place. His other friends had urged him on as well, but losing Sebastian was that last little reminder that at any second it could be too late to get what you want in life. Ansel had become determined to make the most of every moment. In living this way, he felt that same freedom he had felt when he was with Ally. The same freedom that ran through his veins in Philadelphia. He realized it was always in him, that freedom; he had allowed it to slumber for the past twenty-one years. He thought this over as he walked up to the store manager.

"Hello there, handsome," she said cheerfully, adding in a wink. "Can I help you?"

"Hi, I'm Ansel," he beamed. "I think you're in my philosophy class at Hunter Community?" He tried to remain cool and casual.

As the conversation took off, Isabelle and Luca wandered through the market. Within a few moments, Ansel noticed that his friends had reappeared at the cash register adjacent to the one where he and the manager stood flirting. They exchanged numbers as Ansel caught a glimpse of Isabelle, getting buried behind other shoppers. He called her name and she turned around. A rumble came up from what felt like beneath the ground.

Isabelle and the entire store were illuminated by a bright flash, and everything was ablaze. Luca ran toward them, his mouth frozen in a scream as a blast wave tossed them in all up into the air. The vivid hues of red, yellow, orange. A pain like you've never felt, searing, raw, unyielding agony—a calm wave to wash you out to sea. The next moment, Ansel was whole again and in Luca's car with everyone. He got out sooner than usual this time. He ran over to the market and surveyed the aisles frantically, while the rest of the gang took their time. Isabelle entranced with her mangoes. Luca dazzled by the honeydew. Ansel bumped into the store manager.

"Hey, what's going on?" Ansel panicked. The sweat trickling down his forehead felt real, but he couldn't be too certain. He had after all survived some sort of blast; time somehow repeated itself and brought him to the present moment.

"What do you mean, hun?" she said, still as cheerful as she had been before.

"There was a blast of some sort..." Ansel said, before he was startled by Luca and Isabelle's sudden presence by his side.

"Oh," Isabelle said. "We had hoped that you had come to terms with this by now."

Ansel seemed evermore confused, and so Luca explained it all. This particular grocery market had been the target of a bombing by a self-identified "white Christian incel." It was sadly the latest in a string of domestic terrorist attacks. Apparently, the bomber was in protest of the market's decision to carry new pennyroyal supplements, which can be used as a natural abortifacient. There were a few survivors, but neither Luca, Ansel, nor Isabelle had made it out alive. Their deaths were another tragic case of their being in the wrong place at the wrong time.

"No," Ansel said, shaking. He refused to believe it at first, refused to accept that their exits from the world were so quick and random, but Luca assured him it was reality. Ansel had essentially been reliving the same scene over and over again. They arrived at the market, smoked in the car, and headed out. Luca and Isabelle wandered through the aisles while he flirted with the store manager. These were the same events that had led up to the blast. The only way Ansel could begin his true afterlife was to accept his cause of death and embrace that he was no longer a part of the physical world. "I was supposed to do more. This couldn't be it," Ansel sobbed.

"Ansel," said an old familiar voice. It wasn't Luca's voice any longer. In fact, Ansel wasn't even in the grocery market any longer. He looked around and found that he was alone in an all-white room with no doors and no windows. There was no natural source of light in the room, yet everything still glowed as if there was. When the disembodied voice called his name again, this time Ansel instantly recognized it. The voice paralyzed him with disbelief. It was his grandfather.

"Ansel." His grandfather's voice rang out crystal clear. "There are many things you cannot change. You did all that you can, while you could, but you are here now." It was a lesson that had come up all year long. He had witnessed loss in his own family. He had loved Sebastian and lost him to greater opportunities. He had seen how loss had torn at Luca and Ally when Ari died. Now Ansel Wallis realized he had become another love lost himself. Lost to his family, to his ambitions, his future.

His passing was unexpected. He imagined how it would eat at Holly. He longed to go back. He had tried to end it all once, but now that life was truly over, he yearned for nothing more than to live. It was pure irony. Perhaps it was because he had died due to circumstances out of his control. Perhaps he had finally realized all he had to live for. He wasn't sure. All he knew was the desperation, the longing for another sunrise. He had found a job. He had resumed school, but he would never know what was going to come next, and there was nothing he could do about that. That lesson swirled around in his head; sometimes it really is too late. All he had wanted, for the longest time, was to fade into oblivion, and now he finally had. His grandfather's voice echoed in again: "You are here now." Ansel ceased sobbing and took a deep breath. His time had come, and for whatever reason it was now. He dusted himself off and stood up. His granddad's voice called out to him once more, and Ansel followed the voice out of the white room into sheer darkness.

About Hayden Winston

Hayden is a Black, bisexual, novelist, poet and activist. His work draws on his experiences growing up in Los Angeles as a QPOC and the child of West Indian immigrants. He holds a Bachelor of Science in Criminal Justice and resides in Northern California with his husband.

Instagram
www.instagram.com/winston.ink

Facebook
www.facebook.com/haydenws

Website
www.haydenwinston.com

Also from NineStar Press

The Mayor of Oak Street by Vincent Traughber Meis

In the 1960s, Midwestern boy and Boy Scout, Nathan delivers newspapers and mows lawns. Nathan uses his cover to move about yards and sneak into the homes of his neighbors, uncovering their secrets.

In high school, one of the local misfits introduces him to diet pills, which help him overcome his shyness. In an amphetamine high, he meets Cindy, who he hopes will steer him along the "morally straight" path of the Boy Scout Oath he swore to.

Nathan is infatuated with a young doctor down the street, Nicholas (Dr. B), who embodies all the things his mother would love him to be. On one of his secret forays in Dr. B's house, he hides in a closet and witnesses his idol having sex with man while the wife is out of town. Dr. B's affair leads to tragedy, forcing the doctor to leave town.

At college in New Orleans, Nathan meets a group of rebels and expands his drug use. Marc, a bisexual Cajun charmer becomes Nathan's first male sexual experience, but promptly leaves town.

Nathan has a chance encounter with Dr. B, who has moved to New Orleans. Dr. B is in a relationship, but still closeted. Frustrated by Dr. B's cool reaction, Nathan goes on a six-month binge of amphetamines and anonymous sex. On one night of debauchery, he overdoses and ends up in the emergency ward.

Nathan's near death rallies Dr. B and Nathan's other friends to force him into rehab. On the way home from work, Nathan witnesses the gruesome aftermath of the 1973 Up Stairs Lounge fire that devastated the gay population of New Orleans. As a result of the fire, Dr. B's live-in boyfriend leaves town, freeing Dr. B to explore his feelings for Nathan.

Eating the Moon by Mark David Campbell

What if it were the other way around, and homosexuality was the norm and heterosexuals were pushed into the shadows?

During his twice-weekly sessions, Guy, a sixty-seven-year-old anthropologist, tells Richard, his thirty-two-year-old psychiatrist, a fantastic tale about a society where almost everyone is homosexual and sex is considered the most basic form of communication.

As a young man, on a cargo ship that sinks in the Bermuda Triangle, Guy is saved by the first mate, Luca, and they wash up on the shore of an uncharted tropical island. There, Guy must undergo a brutal initiation ritual and swim across shark-infested waters in order to win the love of a local man. Meanwhile, Luca, unable to accept his sexuality, becomes obsessed with being rescued and soon degenerates into drug dependency. Serious trouble ensues when Luca discovers that the locals have a large stash of gold, and he devises a plan to steal it. When Luca's scheme falls apart, Guy must choose between remaining on the island with the man he loves or saving Luca's life.

Could there really be such a society, or does it only exist within the fantasy of a lonely old gay man?

Connect with NineStar Press

www.ninestarpress.com

www.facebook.com/ninestarpress

www.facebook.com/groups/NineStarNiche

www.twitter.com/ninestarpress

www.instagram.com/ninestarpress